VOW OF MALICE

BIANCA COLE

Vow of Malice Copyright © 2026 Bianca Cole

All Rights Reserved.
No part of this publication may be reproduced, stored, or transmitted in any form or by any means, electronic, mechanical, photocopying, recording, scanning, or otherwise without written permission from the publisher. It is illegal to copy this book, post it to a website, or distribute it by any other means without permission.

This novel is entirely a work of fiction. The names, characters and incidents portrayed in it are the work of the author's imagination. Any resemblance to actual persons, living or dead, events or localities is entirely coincidental.

Warning: the unauthorized reproduction or distribution of this copyrighted work is illegal. Criminal copyright infringement, including infringement without monetary gain, is investigated by the FBI and is punishable by up to 5 years in prison and a fine of $250,000.

Edited by: Liana Valerian

CONTENTS

Blurb — v
Playlist — vii
Author's Note — ix

1. Aurora — 1
2. Aurora — 11
3. Hunter — 17
4. Aurora — 23
5. Hunter — 29
6. Aurora — 37
7. Hunter — 45
8. Aurora — 55
9. Hunter — 65
10. Aurora — 73
11. Hunter — 81
12. Hunter — 91
13. Aurora — 101
14. Hunter — 111
15. Aurora — 119
16. Hunter — 127
17. Aurora — 137
18. Hunter — 147
19. Aurora — 153
20. Hunter — 159
21. Aurora — 165
22. Hunter — 177
23. Aurora — 185
24. Hunter — 195
25. Aurora — 203
26. Hunter — 213
27. Aurora — 221

28. Hunter	229
29. Aurora	235
Also by Bianca Cole	245
About the Author	249

BLURB

One glance from Hunter Reed, and my world ignited.

The only problem? He's now my stepsister's fiancé.

A misunderstanding led my stepfather to arrange Hunter's marriage to Olivia, when Hunter had actually been asking about me. Now this ruthless billionaire uses his engagement to invade my life, his touch setting my skin ablaze whenever we're alone.

I should stay away. But as I uncover secrets about Hunter's connection to the shadowy Vipers society, I'm pulled deeper into his dangerous world.

The line between desire and danger blurs with every forbidden moment we share. And at the masquerade ball, when the masks finally come off, I discover the deadliest secret of all.

Was everything between us a lie? Or is the man I shouldn't want the only one who can save me?

PLAYLIST

"Dangerous Hands"— Austin Giorgio
"Don't Mess With My Mind"— EMO
"Mount Everest"— Labrinth
"Boys Like You"— Tanerélle
"Never Enough"—MUNEYLXRD (Feat Meg Myers)
"Tonight"—R3YAN, BLVKES
"Scars"— Boy Epic
"Monsters"— Ruelle
"Shut Up and Listen"—Nicholas Bonnin, Angelicca
"Bad For Me"— I N D I G O, Hailey Grey
"Dirty Mind"— Boy Epic
"Please"— Omido, Ex Habit
"Poison Ivy"— Hemi Moore
"You're The One That I Want"— Lo-Fang

AUTHOR'S NOTE

Hello reader,

This is a warning: this is a **DARK** mafia romance, much like many of my other books, which means there are very sensitive subject matters and dark, triggering content. If you have any triggers, proceed with caution and read the warning below.

As well as a possessive, dominant anti-hero who doesn't take **no** for an answer and a lot of spicy scenes, this book also addresses sensitive subjects. A list of these can be found on my website: www.biancacoleauthor.com

If you have any triggers, then it's best to read the warnings and not proceed. However, if none of these are an issue for you, read on and enjoy this dark romance.

1

AURORA

The mansion looks smaller than I remember. Standing at the wrought-iron gates, I squint up at the sprawling structure perched on the edge of the cliff, its windows reflecting the afternoon sun like dozens of accusing eyes. Twelve years ago, my father walked off that terrace and into the churning water below.

I take a deep breath. What a morbid pilgrimage this is.

After being on a break in Europe since my mom passed last year, I felt the need to come and face this place. To finally stare my fears dead on without mom here to hold my hand.

"Ms. Harrison?" The caretaker appears from around the side of the house, keys jangling. "Everything's ready for your stay."

Harrison. Not my father's name. I became a Harrison after Mom married my stepdad, Derek. Sometimes I wonder if Dad would be hurt knowing I took another man's name, or if he forfeited the right to care when he chose to leave us.

"Thank you." My voice sounds hollow, even to me.

The massive front door groans open, unleashing the smell of lemon polish and a scent of undisturbed air, like walking into a time capsule. The foyer's marble floor echoes beneath my boots, each step amplifying the silence.

To the right, the living room where we'd played board games during storms. To the left, his study where he'd work late into the night; the light under his door was my childhood lighthouse. Straight ahead, the wall of windows frames the endless ocean.

"The cleaning service comes weekly," the caretaker explains, mistaking my stillness for concern about dust. "Mr. Harrison, your stepfather has maintained everything exactly as it was."

I nod, surprised. Derek never mentioned keeping Dad's house intact all these years. What do you preserve in a shrine to suicide? The last place someone wanted to be?

My fingers trail along the banister as I climb the stairs. Photos line the wall of Mom with her beautiful smile, me missing my front teeth, and Dad looking progressively more hollow-eyed as the timeline advances. The happy family we were supposed to be.

The main bedroom door is closed. I reach for the handle, then let my hand fall. Not yet.

Instead, I walk to the terrace doors at the end of the hall and push them open. The salt-laden wind whips my hair across my face as I step outside. Below, waves crash against jagged rocks, constant and eternal.

I step away from the terrace and follow the stone path that winds toward the cliff's edge. A drizzle has begun, misting my face and dampening my hair. I don't bother going back for a jacket. The cold feels right, somehow. Cleansing.

The path grows narrower, slicker with each step. My

boots sink slightly into the mud as I approach the spot where the property ends, and nothing but air exists. The ocean below is angry today, churning and frothing against the rocks. Did Dad hear this same roar before he stepped off? Did he hesitate, even for a second?

I inch closer, peering over the edge. The drop is dizzying, at least two hundred feet down to the jagged rocks and violent surf. My toes reach the very precipice, tiny bits of dirt and stone skittering down the cliffside as I shift my weight. To feel what he felt. To understand.

The rain intensifies, making the ground treacherous. I sway slightly, a strange vertigo taking hold.

Suddenly, strong hands grip my shoulders, yanking me backward with such force that I stumble and fall against a solid chest. The impact steals my breath, while warmth seeps through soaked fabric.

"What the hell do you think you're doing?" a deep voice demands, rougher than the storm around us.

I twist around in his arms, my hands pressing against a chest that doesn't yield. "Get your hands off me!"

He releases me immediately but stays close. His tall frame blocks my path back to the edge, rain darkening his hair to a deep brown, water dripping down a face that's all sharp angles and barely contained fury.

"Who are you?" I demand, trying to ignore how my pulse hammers where his fingers had gripped. "You're trespassing."

"I was about to say the same thing." His eyes narrow, assessing me with an intensity that makes heat pool low in my belly despite the cold rain. "I own the property next door. I saw someone at the cliff's edge in the rain and thought..." He doesn't finish the sentence, but his jaw clenches.

"You thought I was going to jump?" The realization hits like a slap.

He shrugs, unapologetic, those gray-blue eyes never leaving mine. "It looked that way from where I stood."

"Well, I wasn't." The defensive edge in my voice betrays me. Was I? No. Just... looking. Understanding.

"I wasn't going to jump," I repeat, my voice steadier this time. Rain plasters my hair to my face, and I push it back with trembling fingers that have nothing to do with the cold.

The stranger studies me, doubt etched in the furrow between his brows. He takes a step closer, and I'm acutely aware of how my soaked clothes cling to my body, how his gaze drops for a fraction of a second before snapping back to my face.

"Then what exactly were you doing standing at the edge of a cliff in the rain?"

I look past him toward the churning water below, but it isn't easy to focus on anything except his proximity. "Someone close to me jumped from here twelve years ago. I was eight." The words taste like salt on my tongue. "I've been trying to understand why ever since."

Something shifts in his expression, not quite softening, but a flicker of recognition. His eyes, gray as the storm clouds gathering above us, hold mine with an intensity that makes my breath catch.

"Understanding why someone leaves isn't the same as following them," he says, his voice dropping lower.

Lightning cracks across the sky, illuminating his face for an instant. Strong jaw, rain-slicked skin, intensity radiating from every angle of his body. My heart pounds against my ribs in a rhythm that has nothing to do with fear or grief.

"I know the difference," I snap, but heat rushes to my

cheeks, betraying me. I take a step back, suddenly aware of how close we're standing. We're close enough that I can feel the warmth of his body despite the rain.

"Do you?" He moves forward, closing the distance I'd created. An electric current passes between us, making the hair on my arms stand on end. His gaze drops to my mouth, lingers there long enough to make my lips part.

I should step back again. I don't.

"You don't know anything about me," I whisper, my voice barely audible over the storm.

"I know you're standing in the exact spot where your life changed forever." He leans in, his breath warm against my rain-chilled skin. "That's not a place anyone should revisit alone."

The air between us thickens, charged with something that has nothing to do with the lightning overhead. I can see water droplets clinging to his lashes, the storm reflected in his eyes. His hand comes up, fingers brushing a strand of wet hair from my face, and the touch sends electricity skating across my skin.

"Maybe I want to be alone," I manage, but it comes out breathless, unconvincing.

"Liar." The word is soft, almost tender, and he's so close now I can feel the ghost of his breath against my lips. His other hand finds my waist, not pulling, just... resting there. A question.

My hands find his chest again, but this time I'm not pushing away. I'm gripping his soaked shirt, holding on as the world tilts around us. His thumb traces slow circles against my hip through the wet fabric, and I feel that touch everywhere.

"We don't even know each other," I breathe, but I'm

tilting my face up, drawn by some magnetic force I can't name.

"No," he agrees, his nose brushing against mine, lips hovering so close I can almost taste him. "We don't."

The rain pounds around us, but all I can focus on is the fraction of an inch between our mouths, the warmth of his breath mingling with mine, the way his fingers flex against my waist like he's restraining himself from pulling me closer.

I rise onto my toes, closing the distance until our lips are a whisper apart. Barely touching, just the promise of contact, the ghost of a kiss that makes my entire body ache with want.

His hand slides into my wet hair, cradling the back of my head, and I feel him tremble. We stay like that, suspended in the moment, breathing each other's air, lips barely grazing in a touch that's somehow more intimate than any kiss I've ever experienced.

Thunder crashes overhead, breaking the spell.

He pulls back first, just inches, his eyes dark with something that makes my stomach flip. "You should go inside," he says, his voice rough. "Before you catch your death out here."

The loss of his warmth feels like a physical blow.

I step back and cross my arms over my chest. I'm not sure if it's to ward off the cold or to hide how hard I'm breathing. "You don't get to tell me what to do."

A ghost of a smile touches his lips. "No," he agrees, his gaze raking over me once more with undisguised heat. "I don't."

Our eyes lock, and for a moment, the roar of the ocean fades. There's only the rain between us, the inexplicable pull that makes me want to close the distance again even as warning bells sound in my head.

I break away first, turning toward the house before I do something foolish. "Thank you for your concern, but I can handle myself."

"You're welcome to believe that," he says, and I can hear the amusement in his tone. "But I'd suggest staying away from cliff edges during rainstorms." A pause, heavy with unspoken meaning. "Among other dangerous things."

I don't turn around, don't trust myself to look at him again. My lips still tingle from the almost-kiss, my body still hums with unfulfilled electricity.

"It's fine," I manage, still unsettled by the intensity of our encounter and how badly I'd wanted him to close that final fraction of distance. "Thank you for... checking."

He doesn't respond immediately, and I can feel his gaze on my back like a physical touch. Finally, I hear his footsteps in the mud, moving away. I risk a glance over my shoulder and watch him move through the rain, noting the straight line of his shoulders, the confident set of his stride. Despite the weather, he doesn't hurry or hunch against the downpour. The property line between my father's land and his neighbor's is marked by a low stone wall, which he vaults over effortlessly.

Before disappearing down the slope, he turns back. Even across the distance, I feel the weight of his stare, the promise in it.

Then he's gone.

I stand there longer than I should, rain soaking through my clothes, trying to process what just happened. My fingers touch my lips; lips that had been a breath away from his. Why is my heart still beating so rapidly? I'm already wondering when I'll see him again.

. . .

HOURS LATER, after a hot shower that did nothing to wash away the memory of his touch, I sit at the kitchen table while Martha, the housekeeper whom Derek employs to look after the place permanently, cooks dinner. I told her I could handle it, but she insisted on staying to make a home-cooked meal. The smell of her famous pot roast fills the kitchen, but I can barely focus on it. All I can think about is the ghost of a stranger's breath against my mouth, the way his fingers had felt against my waist.

"You must be half-starved," she fusses, ladling gravy over my plate. "Running around in the rain like that. You could catch your death."

"I met the neighbor," I say, picking up my fork with fingers that still feel unsteady. "Tall guy, dark hair. Intimidating."

Martha freezes, serving spoon hovering midair. "You met Hunter Reed?"

The name registers immediately. Everyone knows Hunter Reed, tech billionaire, notorious recluse, rumored to be as ruthless as he is brilliant. My fork clatters against the plate.

"That was Hunter Reed?"

"Must be. He bought the Jenkins estate last year."

"Hunter Reed," I repeat, turning the name over in my mind. The image floods back with startling clarity. I can see him standing in the rain, water sliding down his face, those gray-blue eyes fixed on mine. His mouth hovering over mine, the restraint in every trembling muscle. The way he'd looked at me like he wanted to devour me.

Martha nods, setting down a basket of fresh rolls. "He doesn't come here often. Keeps to himself when he does."

"What do you know about him?" I try to keep my voice casual, but something in Martha's expression tells me I'm failing. My cheeks flush hot at the memory of his hands on me.

"Not much," she says, though her tone suggests otherwise. "Your stepfather deals with him occasionally. Business matters." She hesitates, then adds with a knowing look, "He's not married or engaged, if that's what you're wondering."

Heat flushes my cheeks darker. "I wasn't—"

Martha's knowing smile stops my protest. "He lives primarily in the city. Has a fancy penthouse downtown, same neighborhood as your father's place. This is just his getaway."

I take a bite of pot roast to hide my embarrassment, but I can't taste it. Since our encounter, Hunter's face keeps appearing in my mind. His rain-slicked hair, the commanding presence he had, the way he'd pulled me back from the edge without hesitation. The way he'd almost kissed me, that torturous breath of space between our lips. There was something magnetic about him that I can't shake. Something dangerous.

"He thought I was going to jump," I murmur, more to myself than Martha.

"Were you?" Martha's voice is gentle, concerned.

"No." I look up sharply. "I was just... trying to understand."

Martha's hand covers mine briefly. "Some things can't be understood, dear. Only accepted."

I nod, but my thoughts have already drifted back to Hunter Reed. The way he'd said, *Understanding why someone leaves isn't the same as following them.* Like he'd somehow seen straight through me. The way his thumb had traced circles against my hip. The dark promise in his eyes.

"He seemed... intense," I say, attempting nonchalance and failing miserably.

Martha chuckles. "That's putting it mildly. The man has built an empire from nothing. They say he's brilliant but ruthless." She refills my water glass. "Not someone to trifle with."

I should be repelled by that description. Instead, all I can think about is how his lips had felt ghosting against mine, how badly I'd wanted him to close that final distance. How badly I still want it.

Like a moth to a dangerous flame.

And I've never been good at staying away from things that might burn me.

2

AURORA

After my encounter with Hunter Reed at the cliff house, I spent two more days there before heading back to New York. The Harrison estate looms before me as my taxi pulls through the wrought iron gates. It looks the same with its imposing stone façade and manicured gardens.

The driver helps with my bags, and I stand for a moment in the circular driveway, taking in the place I grew up but haven't visited in months. Europe had been my escape—art galleries in Paris, cobblestone streets in Prague, anything to distance myself from Mom's empty hospital room and the hollow feeling she left behind. Then the cliff house, where everything began and ended. Where Hunter's hands had steadied me.

Before I can reach for the door, it flies open.

"Aurora!" Olivia launches herself at me in a flurry of expensive perfume and designer clothes. My sister wraps her arms around me so tightly I can barely breathe. "You're finally home! I've been texting you for days!"

Despite my emotional exhaustion, I can't help but smile

as I hug her back. "I was at Dad's cliff house. Service is terrible there."

Liv pulls back, her perfectly manicured hands gripping my shoulders. "The cliff house? Why would you go there?" Her eyes narrow with concern. "That place is nothing but bad memories."

"It was the anniversary," I say simply. She knows what I mean.

Her expression softens. "You should have told me. I would have gone with you."

"I needed to be alone." The memory of Hunter's intense gaze flashes through my mind. Well, not entirely alone. I couldn't stop thinking about him, but he never resurfaced again during the two days I spent there.

"Well, you're home now." Liv links her arm through mine, practically vibrating with excitement as she pulls me inside. "And I have the biggest news ever. You won't believe what happened while you were gone!"

Liv drags me through the foyer. "Dad's waiting in the dining room. He's been asking about you all day, you know."

"Is that my Aurora I hear?" Derek's voice carries from down the hall.

My heart warms at the sound. He's not my biological father, but he's been "Dad" since he married Mom when I was eight. After losing both my birth father and, just last year, my mother, Derek has been my rock.

We enter the dining room where he's already standing, arms outstretched. His silver-flecked dark hair is perfectly styled as always, his custom suit impeccable despite the late hour.

"There she is." His embrace feels like home—steady and secure. He holds me at arm's length, his eyes searching mine. "You look tired, sweetheart. Europe wasn't enough of a break?"

"I stopped at the cliff house on my way back," I admit.

Understanding crosses his face. He doesn't press for details, just nods and squeezes my shoulder. "I'm glad you're home. Alice made your favorite."

The table is set for three, but it's not the formal dining setup we use for business associates or society events. Tonight, we're gathered at the smaller breakfast nook with its bay windows overlooking the gardens. Candles flicker between plates of roasted chicken, creamy risotto, and fresh vegetables.

"Wine, Aurora?" Derek reaches for the bottle of Chardonnay.

"Please."

Olivia fidgets in her seat, clearly bursting to share her news but playing along with the routine of our family dinner first. We fall into our familiar rhythm—passing dishes, sharing bites, the conversation flowing easily.

"The Harrison Foundation gala exceeded our fundraising goal," Derek mentions, pride evident in his voice. "The children's hospital will get its new wing."

"That's wonderful," I say, feeling a twinge of guilt for missing it.

"Aurora contributed the most beautiful piece for the auction," Liv adds, smiling at me. "Your painting of the Italian coastline went for double the estimated value."

"Really?" I feel a spark of pride. My art has always been a private passion.

Derek raises his glass. "To my two incredibly talented daughters."

As we clink glasses, I realize how much I've missed this

—the three of us, together. Whatever storm clouds gather outside our family circle, in here, we're just us.

Liv can barely contain herself any longer, tucking her perfectly highlighted blonde hair behind one ear—a gesture I recognize as her trying to hold back excitement. We couldn't look more different if we tried. She's all polished elegance in her cream cashmere sweater, while I'm still in the same jeans and oversized sweater I wore on the plane.

After we toast, Derek turns his attention to Liv. "Now, I think your sister is dying to hear your news."

"Yes!" Liv claps her hands together. "Daddy approved my proposal for the new social media campaign for Harrison Industries! I'm going to be the face of the youth outreach initiative!"

I smile, genuinely happy for her. While I've chosen art and independence, Liv has always embraced her role as the Harrison heiress, polishing her public persona to mirror Dad's business values.

"That's amazing, Liv," I say, raising my glass again. "Nobody could represent the company better."

"It's going to be incredible," she continues, eyes bright with excitement. "Full creative control, my own team. Daddy says it's time the company appealed to a younger demographic."

Derek beams with pride. "Olivia presented a comprehensive strategy that impressed even the board's most conservative members. Our little social butterfly is showing her business acumen."

Liv glows under his praise. "I've already started planning the launch event. Which reminds me—" She turns to me, "—I'm going to need your help. I want to feature local artists, and you have all the right connections."

"Of course," I agree, surprised but pleased she wants my involvement.

"And there's something else," Liv adds, lowering her voice dramatically. "I met a guy I like."

Dad raises an eyebrow. "Oh?"

"It's nothing yet," she says quickly. "But he's... different. In a good way."

"Anyone I know?" I ask, curious about who could have caught my sister's discerning eye.

"Maybe. I don't want to jinx it by saying too much too soon." She taps her perfectly manicured nails against her wine glass. "He hasn't even asked me out."

While we finish dessert, Liv can't seem to contain herself any longer about her mystery man. Her eyes sparkle with a light I haven't seen before.

"Okay, I can't stand it. I have to tell you more about him." She leans forward, lowering her voice conspiratorially. "His name is Ari. We met at the charity auction for the children's hospital."

"Ari." I repeat the name, trying to place it. "Wasn't he part of that tech investment group that Dad works with sometimes?"

Derek sets down his fork. "Ari Carter? From Vipers Ventures?"

"Yes!" Liv's cheeks flush. "He was there representing their philanthropic division. We started talking about social media outreach strategies for nonprofits, and then..." She trails off, biting her lip. "We've been texting each other almost every day since."

"Isn't he a little... old for you?" Derek asks, his brow furrowing slightly.

Liv shakes her head. "That's what makes him different. He isn't immature like guys my age." She gestures vaguely around the dining room. "He actually challenged me on some of my ideas for the campaign. Made them better. No one does that."

I watch my sister carefully. This isn't her usual gushing about a handsome face or impressive credentials. There's something vulnerable in her expression.

"He and I had a great conversation the other day," she continues. "He brought up something I mentioned in passing last week. He actually listens when I talk."

"That sounds promising," I say, genuinely happy for her if this does work out, as she has had her fair share of bums. "Does he know about your Instagram influencer status?"

Liv laughs. "He teases me about it. Says my followers don't know the real Olivia Harrison." Her voice softens. "Sometimes I think he might be right. There's more to me than perfect posts and charity galas."

I reach across the table and squeeze her hand. "I've always known that, Liv."

The conversation shifts to my travels, and I find myself relaxing into the familiar embrace of family. For tonight at least, the strange encounter at the cliff and the mysterious Hunter Reed feel distant, like something from another life.

3

HUNTER

I adjust my cufflinks for the third time as the Harrison mansion comes into view through the car window. For two weeks, I haven't been able to shake the image of Harrison's daughter standing in the rain, her face turned toward the sky, so close to the edge that a single misstep would have sent her plummeting. The vulnerability in her eyes, the quiet defiance in her voice, all of it has been playing on a loop in my mind.

"We've arrived, sir," my driver announces, pulling up to the circular driveway.

The board made itself abundantly clear. My "Playboy lifestyle" was becoming a liability for shareholders. The constant rotation of models and actresses damaged our family-friendly image. Their solution? Marriage. Stability. Respectability.

Meeting Derek Harrison's daughter on that cliff edge came at exactly the right moment. From my research, I quickly learned that the woman in question is Derek's daughter, Olivia. And a merger with our companies would satisfy the shareholders in more than one way. A business arrangement, a stop to my "Playboy lifestyle", and I get the woman I've become obsessed with. It's a win all around.

"Hunter!" Derek greets me at the door with a broad smile and firm handshake. "Right on time."

"Derek." I return his handshake, stepping into the grand foyer. "Thank you for the invitation."

"Olivia's so excited to meet you." He lowers his voice conspiratorially. "Between us, she's been following your career for years."

I smile. "I look forward to meeting her." Even though I had already met her on that cliff.

The living room is filled with members of the Harrison family and close friends, all impeccably dressed. I scan the room, mentally cataloging faces, but I don't see her.

A blonde girl approaches me, champagne flute in hand. "Hunter, isn't it?" She kisses the air beside my cheek. "I'm Olivia, it's so lovely to meet you."

My stomach drops. This isn't the girl from the cliff. Sure, she's objectively beautiful with blonde hair styled in perfect waves, designer dress showcasing a slim figure. Yet I find myself searching the room again, looking for that dark hair and azure eyes.

Who was she if she wasn't Derek's daughter?

The entire reason I considered marrying Derek Harrison's daughter was that I believed it was her.

"The pleasure's mine," I respond mechanically.

"Dinner will be served soon, but first," Derek's voice cuts through the conversation as he addresses the room. "I'd like everyone to meet my stepdaughter, Aurora, who's finally back after her time away."

My body freezes as a woman approaches.

It's her.

The woman from the cliff edge stands across the room,

and our eyes lock. Time freezes. Recognition flashes across her face, quickly replaced by something deeper, more intense. It's the same electric chemistry I felt that night, only stronger now, confirming that our connection wasn't just my imagination.

She holds my gaze without flinching. No polite smile, no demure glance away. She meets my gaze with unflinching intensity that makes my blood run hot.

"Hunter, I'd like you to meet my stepdaughter, Aurora," Derek says, completely oblivious to the current passing between us. "Aurora, this is Hunter Reed, CEO of Reed Technologies."

My jaw clenches so hard I feel my teeth might crack. I pride myself on knowing everything about everyone in my orbit. Yet somehow, I missed that Derek Harrison is still in touch with his stepdaughter.

Aurora approaches with measured steps, her expression neutral. "Mr. Reed and I have already met, Dad."

Derek raises his eyebrows. "Oh? I wasn't aware."

"Briefly," I interject, my voice clipped. "At the cliff house."

My mind races through all the information I've gathered about Derek. The cliff house was purchased after his marriage to Margaret, Aurora's mother, I'm now piecing together. Aurora had mentioned that someone close to her had jumped. She must have meant her biological father.

I should have known. I should have found her the moment I started looking.

"Small world," Derek says with a chuckle, completely missing the tension. "Hunter, I'm hoping to discuss the Westview development after dinner. I think there's potential for our companies to partner there."

I nod, barely hearing him. Aurora hasn't broken eye

contact, challenging me with her gaze. "Yes, small world indeed."

"I'd like everyone's attention," Derek announces, tapping his glass with a silver spoon. The room quiets immediately, all eyes turning toward our host. "Hunter and I have an important announcement to make."

The words snap me back to reality. My gaze breaks from Aurora's.

Fuck.

The woman on the cliff edge wasn't Olivia Harrison, the woman I've agreed to marry, as well as securing a huge merger. The contract is practically signed, and it not only impacts me but the Vipers too.

And now I learn that Olivia is not the woman I wanted.

Olivia appears at my side, sliding her hand into mine. I resist the urge to snatch it away, to wipe my palm against my suit after her touch. She's nothing but a means to an end.

"As many of you know," Derek continues, "Hunter and I have been associates for years. Tonight, we're thrilled to announce that the association is becoming much more permanent."

I study Aurora's face. The slight widening of her eyes. The almost imperceptible tightening of her jaw. My mind categorizes and files away each expression for later analysis.

She will be mine.

The room erupts in applause as Derek concludes his announcement. I offer a practiced smile, shake hands, and accept congratulations. All while part of my brain calculates how to extricate myself from this arrangement without damaging the business interests at stake.

Interesting how these pieces have arranged themselves

on the board. Finding out Aurora is not the woman I'm engaged to marry changes everything. I'll adjust the game.

Olivia squeezes my hand, beaming up at me. "Isn't this wonderful?"

"Perfect," I reply, mentally relegating her to the category of "obstacles to be removed." Not physically because I'm not an animal, and I sense Aurora would never forgive me. But obstacles have solutions. People have pressure points. Everything and everyone can be controlled with the right leverage.

And I've never encountered a problem I couldn't solve.

4

AURORA

The sleek black town car glides through downtown traffic, carrying Olivia and me toward Elixir, the newest upscale cocktail lounge everyone's been raving about. The city lights blur outside the window as I stare at them, trying to process everything that happened at dinner. Hunter Reed. The way his eyes locked with mine. The announcement.

My stomach twists again. I turn to Olivia, who's texting furiously, probably updating Chloe and Daisy about our ETA.

"So," I say, keeping my voice casual. "When exactly were you planning to tell me you are getting engaged to Hunter Reed?"

Olivia looks up from her phone, guilt flashing across her face. "I wanted to tell you, Aurora. I really did."

"But you didn't." The hurt in my voice surprises even me. "How long have you known?"

She sighs, tucking a strand of perfectly highlighted hair behind her ear. "About one week. Hunter approached him two weeks ago, apparently. Some kind of merger or partnership thing." She rolls her eyes. "You know how Dad is with his business arrangements."

Two weeks ago. When we first met.

"A week?" My voice rises. "And you didn't think to mention it to me? Your sister?"

"Dad made me promise not to tell anyone. He wanted to make the announcement himself." Olivia reaches for my hand. "He said it was important for the business that nothing leaked before everything was finalized."

"Anyone?" I pull my hand away. "Even me? Since when does Dad keep me out of family decisions?"

Olivia winces. "I know. I felt terrible keeping it from you. But Dad was super serious about it. He said Hunter insisted on complete confidentiality until the announcement."

The mention of his name sends an unwelcome shiver through me. I turn back to the window, watching raindrops race down the glass.

"It's just…" I hesitate. "Dad always includes me in everything. Even the business stuff that doesn't directly involve me."

"I know," Olivia says softly. "I think it's because you've been dealing with grief over your mom and just returning to New York. He didn't want to burden you with more."

Her words sting because they make sense. My stepdad has been overly careful with me since my mom died, treating me like I might break.

The car pulls up to the curb outside Elixir, where a line of well-dressed people waits under the glow of blue neon.

"They're already inside," Olivia says, checking her phone. "Chloe has got us a table."

We push through the crowded entrance, and I spot Chloe's vibrant blue hair immediately. She's waving frantically from a corner booth, Daisy sitting quietly beside her.

"Finally!" Chloe jumps up, pulling us both into a hug that smells like expensive perfume and top-shelf vodka. "I thought you'd never get here!"

We slide into the booth, and a server immediately appears with drinks. A pink cocktail for Olivia and a whiskey neat for me. Chloe must have already ordered for us.

"Tell us everything about the engagement!" Chloe demands, her colorful cocktail matching her vibrant personality. She leans forward, eyes sparkling with excitement. "Every. Single. Detail."

"He's absolutely perfect," Olivia gushes, her face lighting up. "Powerful, wealthy, and those eyes!" She fans herself dramatically. "I mean, have you ever seen eyes that shade?"

I take a long sip of whiskey, welcoming the burn down my throat. The memory of those same eyes locked on mine at the cliff edge makes my skin prickle with heat.

"Dad says it'll be the marriage of the century," Olivia continues. "The wedding's set for next spring at the vineyard."

Daisy slides closer to me on the bench, her quiet presence somehow steadying. While Olivia details wedding plans and Chloe peppers her with questions, Daisy nudges me gently.

"Are you okay?" she whispers, her voice barely audible over the lounge music.

"Just tired," I lie, forcing a smile while guilt churns in my stomach. I can't tell anyone about the electricity I felt with Hunter. About how wrong it is that I can't stop thinking about my sister's fiancé.

Chloe suddenly straightens in her seat, subtly nodding toward the bar. "Ladies, don't look now, but I think we have admirers."

"You think everyone's an admirer," Daisy says with a small smile.

"That's because everyone is," Chloe fires back, tossing her blue hair. "The tall one hasn't taken his eyes off Aurora since we walked in."

"Maybe he's just jealous of my whiskey," I say, grateful for the distraction.

I glance over at the bar, following Chloe's not-so-subtle head tilt. The man is leaning against the polished surface, drink in hand, his gaze indeed fixed on us. Tall, with broad shoulders and the kind of jawline that belongs on a movie poster. Objectively handsome in his tailored navy suit, clearly expensive from the way it fits his athletic frame.

Our eyes meet. He smiles, confidence radiating from him as he raises his glass slightly in acknowledgment.

I should feel something. A flutter. A spark. Any normal woman would.

But there's nothing. Just... emptiness.

Unlike the spark that shot through me when Hunter's storm-gray eyes locked with mine. Unlike the way my skin burned where his fingers gripped my arm at the cliff edge.

I turn away, taking another burning swallow of whiskey. What the hell is wrong with me? The gorgeous guy at the bar practically has "eligible bachelor" stamped on his forehead, while Hunter Reed is my stepsister's fiancé. My SISTER. The man is literally taken, announced to the world tonight as Olivia's future husband.

And here I am, unable to forget the way he looked at me, like he was memorizing every detail of my face.

"Aurora?" Olivia nudges me, breaking my spiral of self-loathing. "You didn't hear a word I said, did you?"

"Sorry," I mutter, forcing myself back to the conversation. "Just distracted."

"I was asking if you'll help with the wedding planning," she repeats, excitement coloring her voice. "You have such good taste."

My stomach drops. Planning my sister's wedding to the only man who's made me feel alive in years.

Fuck my life.

I drain my whiskey, welcoming the burn. "Of course I will," I hear myself say, the perfect supportive sister, while my insides twist with guilt.

5

HUNTER

The bass thrums through Elixir's walls as I descend the private staircase to the VIP section. Our section. The place where the Vipers conduct business is away from prying eyes, hidden behind one-way glass and soundproofing that costs more than most people's houses.

Penn's already holding court at our usual table, surrounded by bottles of top-shelf liquor and the kind of women who know better than to ask questions. He spots me immediately, that wild grin splitting his face.

"There he is!" Penn shouts over the music. "The man of the fucking hour! Or should I say, the engaged man?"

I flip him off as I drop into the booth beside Ari, who's nursing what looks like a glass of scotch and scrolling through his phone with that lazy elegance he's perfected.

"Congratulations are in order, I hear," Ari drawls without looking up. "Derek Harrison's daughter. Quite the catch."

"Which one?" Blaze asks from across the table, his scarred knuckles wrapped around a beer bottle. "Heard he's got two."

My jaw clenches. "Olivia. The socialite."

"The boring one," Penn laughs, pouring himself another shot. "I've met her at charity galas. Pretty enough, but Christ, she could bore a man to death."

Grayson leans back in his seat, dark eyes assessing me with that unnerving perception he's always had. "You don't look like a man celebrating his engagement."

"Because I'm here celebrating Penn's birthday, asshole," I fire back.

"Thirty and still devastatingly handsome," Penn says, raising his glass. "Unlike you, stuck with a soon-to-be wife who probably alphabetizes her closet."

"Better than your collection of one-night stands who don't know your real last name," Ari murmurs, finally setting his phone down.

I reach for the whiskey bottle, pouring three fingers and downing half in one swallow. The image of Aurora standing at that cliff edge burns behind my eyes. The rain plastered her dark hair to her face. Those azure eyes full of pain and defiance and something that called to every dark part of me.

"Hunt's awfully quiet," Blaze observes. "Usually, you'd have something to say about Penn's dating habits."

"Just thinking about business," I lie.

"Business." Grayson's tone suggests he doesn't believe a word. "Right."

Penn leans forward, eyes glittering with mischief and alcohol. "Come on. Tell us. What's the unlucky bride-to-be like? Besides terminally dull?"

Wrong sister, I think, downing the rest of my whiskey. *Very wrong fucking sister.*

"It's business," I snap, refilling my glass. "Nothing

more. Derek needed an alliance; the board wants stability. Done."

"Romantic," Penn snorts.

I level him with a look that's ended lesser men. "Since when do we give a shit about romance?"

"Fair point." He raises his glass in mock salute.

Ari's still watching me with those sharp eyes, seeing more than I want him to. I need to redirect this conversation before he starts picking apart my body language like the nosy bastard he is.

"Speaking of business," I say, leaning back and letting my gaze sweep the club below. "Selection's coming up. Two weeks."

The energy at the table shifts immediately. This is familiar territory. Safe ground.

"About fucking time," Penn says, straightening. "We've had the same deadweight for three years. Need fresh blood."

"Fresh blood that actually knows what they're doing," Blaze adds. "Last batch was shit."

Grayson sets down his drink. "I've been vetting candidates. Got it narrowed to fifteen possibles."

"Fifteen?" Ari raises an eyebrow. "We only need five positions filled."

"Which means we choose the best at selection and cut the rest," I say. "No room for weakness."

"Some interesting prospects this year," Grayson continues. "Congressman's son with a taste for insider trading. Tech mogul's daughter who's been running her own hacking operation. A few others with the right... moral flexibility."

"The congressman's kid, that Thompson's boy?" Penn asks. "I met him at a fundraiser. Spineless little shit."

"Money doesn't discriminate based on spine," I point out. "Question is whether he can handle the work."

"We'll find out during trials," Blaze says, cracking his knuckles. "Always do."

The trials. Two weeks of testing candidates' limits and their loyalty, their ruthlessness, their ability to keep their mouths shut when it matters. Some wash out. Some break. The ones who make it through earn their place at the table.

"Are we doing the usual format?" Ari asks.

I nod. "Physical tests with Blaze. Social manipulation with Ari. Criminal operations with Grayson. Penn handles the psychological pressure."

"My favorite part," Penn grins, that manic edge creeping into his expression.

"And what about you?" Blaze asks, turning his attention my way. "What's your role this year?"

I swirl the whiskey in my glass, watching the amber liquid catch the light. "The same as always."

Penn's grin widens. "Ah, yes. The fun part."

Ari shifts beside me. "Hunter handles the breaking point."

"Because he's so good at it," Grayson adds, no judgment in his tone. Just a fact.

They're not wrong. While Blaze tests physical limits and Penn toys with psychological pressure, I handle what comes after—when candidates think they've survived the worst. When they start to relax, believing they've proven themselves.

That's when I step in.

"Last year's batch was disappointing," I say, remembering the congressman's aide who'd pissed himself before I'd even started. "Thought they were tough until they saw the room."

"The room" is the soundproofed basement beneath one of my properties. The one with drain grates in the concrete floor and walls that don't show stains. I find out exactly how far someone will go when pushed past every reasonable limit.

"You broke that investment banker in twenty minutes," Penn recalls with something like admiration. "Thought he'd last longer."

"He talked too much. Tried to negotiate." I drain my glass. "In our world, you do what needs doing. No hesitation. No conscience getting in the way."

"And you have no conscience to get in the way," Ari observes mildly.

"Which is why I'm good at it."

Blaze leans forward. "We need candidates who won't flinch when things get bloody. Last thing we need is someone who'll fall apart during an actual operation."

"Exactly." I pour another drink. "They can pass every other test, but if they can't handle what I put them through, they're useless to us."

"How many do you think will make it through this year?" Grayson asks.

I consider the question. "Maybe three. If we're lucky."

"Out of fifteen?" Penn laughs. "Harsh."

"Better harsh than dead." I meet his eyes. "One weak link in the chain and we all hang."

The mood shifts. Penn's wild grin fades. Ari stops twirling his glass. Even Grayson's expression hardens.

Because it's the truth none of us say out loud often, even among ourselves.

The Vipers isn't some gentleman's club or networking group for the elite. It's a machine built on blood, blackmail, and the kind of connections that make politicians nervous and law enforcement look the other way.

We control everything that matters in this city. Every development deal, every election, every piece of legislation that affects our interests. And we do it through methods that would make most people sick.

"Remember why we started this," Blaze says finally, his voice low. "We were kids who saw how the world really worked. Saw that power wasn't about money or family name."

"It was about being willing to do what others wouldn't," I finish.

Ari shifts beside me. "Our parents thought we were networking at that boarding school. Building connections for future business deals."

"Instead, we were learning that laws only apply to people without enough money to ignore them," Penn adds, some of his usual levity returning. "And that morality is just a word the weak use to feel superior. Jax taught us that."

"We helped him build something real," Grayson says. "Something that lasts. But only because we've been careful about who we let in."

I nod, feeling the familiar weight of responsibility settle over my shoulders. We joined the vipers together—college kids who recognized kindred spirits in each other. Who understood that the world was divided between those who took what they wanted and those who got crushed beneath them. At the time, it was in its infancy. The brainchild of Jax King.

Now we're fifty members strong. Politicians, CEOs, judges, police commissioners. The leader, Jax, was like us at the start, but he's allowed the power to get to his head a bit too much. Everyone in the Vipers understands that real power comes from being willing to cross lines others won't approach.

"Selection matters," I say. "Every person we bring in either strengthens us or becomes a liability. There's no middle ground."

"No mercy for weakness," Penn agrees, raising his glass.

"No hesitation when action is needed," Blaze adds.

"No conscience to get in the way," Ari finishes.

Grayson lifts his drink. "To the Vipers."

We all raise our glasses, the ritual grounding. This is who we are, what we've achieved together. The Vipers may not be our organization, but we're fundamental to it. It wouldn't exist without us, and our leader, Jax, knows it.

6

AURORA

The private room at Elixir pulses with bass from the main floor, muffled enough that we can talk without shouting. Chloe's already three cosmoses deep, her bright pink hair catching the neon lights as she gestures wildly.

"I'm just saying, if you're going to get married, at least make sure the sex is good first." She points her glass at Olivia. "You have slept with him, right?"

Olivia's cheeks flush. "That's not—we're taking things slow."

"Slow?" Chloe nearly chokes on her drink. "Babe, you're engaged before the first date. That's not slow."

Grace laughs from her spot on the velvet couch, legs tucked beneath her. "Leave her alone. Some people wait."

"For what? Disappointment?" Chloe grins. "I'm doing you a favor, Liv. Test drive before you buy."

Daisy shakes her head, quiet as always, but there's amusement in her eyes. She sits beside me, nursing a gin and tonic while the chaos swirls around us.

I should be laughing with them. Should be joining in

Chloe's teasing or defending Olivia's choices. Instead, I'm trying not to think about Hunter Reed's hands on my shoulders. The intensity in those dark eyes when he looked at me at their engagement announcement.

"Aurora agrees with me." Chloe turns her attention my way. "Right? You'd want to know what you're getting into?"

"I—" My throat tightens. "I think Olivia should do whatever feels right for her."

Olivia beams at me. "See? Aurora gets it."

Grace arches an eyebrow. "That's unusually diplomatic of you."

Damn. I've been too quiet. Too careful. These women know me well enough to notice when something's off.

"Just tired," I lie, taking a sip of my Manhattan. "It's been a long week."

"Because of your dad's anniversary?" Daisy's voice is soft, but her question cuts straight through.

The others fall quiet. Even Chloe stops mid-drink.

"Yeah." I latch onto the excuse. "Going back there brought up a lot of memories."

Olivia reaches over and squeezes my hand. "I'm sorry I wasn't there with you. I should have been."

Guilt twists in my chest. She's apologizing when I'm the one harboring feelings for her fiancé.

"You had your own stuff going on," I manage.

"Dance with me," Grace says suddenly, standing and extending her hand.

I blink. "What?"

"You heard me. Come on." She wiggles her fingers. "When's the last time you actually let loose?"

"I don't dance." The words come out automatically. I hate dancing—hate the attention, the spectacle of it all.

"Exactly why you should." Grace's dark eyes see too

much. She knows I'm drowning here, suffocating under the weight of Olivia's happiness and my own fucked up attraction to a man I barely know.

A man who's marrying my stepsister.

"Go!" Chloe shoves me forward. "We'll hold down the fort here."

Olivia laughs. "This I must see. Aurora Harrison on the dance floor."

The pressure in my chest intensifies. If I stay here one more minute listening to wedding talk, listening to my sister gush about a future with Hunter, I'm going to crack. Going to say something I can't take back.

"Fine." I grab Grace's hand and let her pull me through the crowd.

The main floor throbs with bodies and heat. EDM pounds through massive speakers, the beat vibrating through my bones. Grace weaves us toward the center, where the mass of people provides cover, anonymity.

"What's going on?" She leans close to my ear to be heard.

"Nothing."

"Bullshit." Grace spins, her movements fluid despite the crush of dancers. "You've been off all night."

I try to match her rhythm, feeling awkward and exposed. "Just stressed."

"About your mom?"

"Sure."

Grace stops moving. Crosses her arms. In the middle of the pulsing dance floor, she stares at me.

"Seriously?" I shout over the music.

"Not moving until you tell me what's actually wrong."

A guy bumps into my back, muttering an apology. The

lights strobe across Grace's face in an array of pink, blue, and green. She doesn't budge.

"It's complicated," I finally admit.

"When isn't it?" She grabs my hands, forcing me to sway with her. "Talk to me, Aurora. You're freaking out about something."

My stomach clenches. I can't tell her. Can't admit that every time Olivia mentions Hunter's name, I feel heat pool low in my belly.

The words stick in my throat. Grace is the only one I could tell. The only one who wouldn't run straight to Olivia with every secret I spill.

I lean closer, lips brushing her ear. "Bathroom. Now."

Her eyes widen, but she nods.

We push through the crowd, Grace leading the way. The bathroom is marginally quieter; the bass has been reduced to a dull thud. Two women touch up their makeup in the mirror. Grace checks under the stall doors, confirms we're otherwise alone.

She crosses her arms and leans against the counter. "Spill."

My hands shake. I grip the edge of the sink beside her, staring at my reflection. Dark hair falling loose around my shoulders. Eyes too bright with panic.

"I met Hunter," I whisper. "About a week before the engagement announcement."

Grace's expression doesn't change. "And?"

"And we," I close my eyes. "We almost kissed."

"Fuck."

"Yeah." I turn to face her. "He pulled me back from the cliff edge at my dad's place. Thought I was going to jump. We were so close, Grace. His hands on my shoulders, his breath on my face. I swear he was going to—"

"Did he know who you were?"

"No. Neither of us did." The words tumble out faster now. "I didn't know he was the neighbor. Didn't know Derek was arranging anything. And then one week later, I'm at the party, and he walks in and is suddenly engaged to Oliva."

Grace's jaw tightens. "Jesus, Aurora."

"I can't stop thinking about him." My voice cracks. "Every time Olivia says his name, I feel it here." I press my hand to my stomach. "And I hate myself for it because she's happy. She's so fucking happy, and I'm..."

"Obsessing over her fiancé."

"Yes." The admission tears out of me.

One of the women at the mirror glances our way. Grace shifts, blocking me from view.

"Do you think he believed the engagement was to you?" Her voice stays low, controlled.

"Maybe?" I grip the counter harder. "The way he looked at me, Grace. Like he knew exactly what I was thinking."

"Do you think he likes you too?" Grace's question cuts through my spiraling thoughts.

I press my fingers against my temples. "I think so..." I shake my head. "But who the hell knows what goes on in that man's head. He's a fucking enigma."

"Hunter Reed doesn't exactly scream transparent," Grace agrees.

The bathroom door swings open. Three giggling women stumble in, clearly drunk. Grace grabs my wrist and pulls me toward the hallway outside.

We find a quieter corner near the emergency exit, away from the pounding bass and the crowd. The metal railing feels cool under my palms as I lean against it.

Grace studies me for a long moment. "You need to tell Olivia."

"What?" My stomach drops. "Are you insane?"

"Listen to me." She steps closer, her voice firm. "It's not like they have some grand romance going on. They barely know each other. Derek arranged the whole thing for business reasons."

"That doesn't matter—"

"It does matter," Grace cuts me off. "Olivia's excited about the wedding and the attention, sure. But there's no emotional bond there. No deep connection. She's marrying him because your dad told her to."

My chest tightens. "And that makes it okay for me to, what? Confess that I'm attracted to her fiancé?"

"It makes it honest." Grace's dark eyes bore into mine. "You think she won't notice something's off? You were practically vibrating with tension all night. Daisy and I picked up on it, and we're not even the ones planning a wedding with you as the maid of honor."

"I can't." The words feel strangled. "Grace, I can't do that to her."

"Can't? Or won't?" She crosses her arms. "Because keeping this secret while you help plan her wedding—that's worse. That's lying every single day."

Heat crawls up my neck. She's right. I know she's right.

"What am I supposed to say?" I push off the railing. "Hey, Liv, remember your fiancé? Yeah, I want to fuck him. Hope that's cool."

"Maybe not those exact words." Grace's lips twitch despite the gravity. "But something close to the truth before this gets worse."

I exhale slowly, the weight of her words settling over me. "You might be right."

"Might?" Grace raises an eyebrow.

"Fine. You are right." I rake my hands through my hair. "But I can't do it tonight. Not when we're all drinking, and she's riding this high about the engagement."

Grace tilts her head, considering.

"I need to tell her when we're both sober," I continue. "When I can actually think straight, and she can process it without cosmos clouding her judgment."

"Okay." Grace's shoulders relax slightly. "That's fair."

Relief floods through me. "Thank you. I just need a few days to figure out how to—"

"One week."

I freeze. "What?"

"You have one week to tell her." Grace's expression hardens. "If you don't, I will."

My stomach drops. "Grace!"

"I'm serious, Aurora. I'm not watching you torture yourself over this for months while Olivia plans a wedding, completely oblivious." She steps closer. "And I'm not keeping secrets from her that affect her life this much."

"That's a little unfair." Heat flashes through me. "You're basically forcing my hand."

"Yes." Grace doesn't flinch. "Because you won't do it otherwise. You'll keep finding excuses, keep putting it off until it's too late and the damage is worse."

"You don't know that."

"Don't I?" She crosses her arms. "How many times have you avoided difficult conversations by telling yourself 'later' or 'when the time is right'? Your mom's cancer diagnosis. Hell, even going back to your dad's house for the first time took you six years."

The words hit like a physical blow. "Low."

"True." Grace's voice softens, but her stance doesn't

waver. "I love you, Aurora, which is exactly why I'm doing this. One week."

My hands ball into fists. Part of me wants to argue, to tell her she has no right to set ultimatums about my life. But the rational part that knows I'm drowning understands she's throwing me a lifeline.

"Fine." The word tastes bitter. "One week."

7

HUNTER

The bass pounds through Elixir's VIP section like a headache set to rhythm. I nurse my whiskey, watching Penn work his way through his third bottle of champagne while Ari entertains some socialite who won't stop touching his arm.

"You're brooding." Penn drops into the seat beside me, his grin sharp. "It's my birthday. Stop being a miserable fuck."

"I'm here, aren't I?"

"Physically." He gestures at my untouched phone on the table. "Mentally, you're locked in that fortress of yours, planning world domination or whatever the hell you do."

"Something like that."

Ari extracts himself from the socialite and slides into the booth across from us. "You know, most people would be celebrating an engagement. Buying rounds. Making a spectacle."

"I'm not most people."

"No shit." Penn refills his glass, champagne sloshing over the rim. "You're the poor bastard who agreed to marry

Olivia Harrison for a merger. At least pretend to enjoy yourself."

Movement catches my eye across the club.

Dark hair. Azure eyes. That same defiant tilt to her chin I saw on the cliff.

Aurora.

She's crossing the main floor with another woman who has a dark complexion and a confident stride. They're heading toward the bar area, weaving through the crowd. Aurora says something that makes her companion laugh, throwing her head back.

Every muscle in my body tenses.

"Hunt?" Ari's voice sounds distant.

I track Aurora's path, cataloging every detail. The way her dress hugs her curves. How she scans the room like she's searching for something. The protective edge to how the other woman walks beside her. From their body language, I ascertain she's a friend, and a close one.

They're moving toward the VIP section.

Where Olivia sits with two other women, champagne glasses raised in some toast.

Fuck.

Aurora slides into the booth beside my fiancée, accepting a drink from one of the others. The friend she was walking through the crowd with settles on her other side. They're laughing about something, the whole group animated and bright.

Olivia throws an arm around Aurora's shoulders, pulling her close.

My jaw clenches so hard my teeth ache.

"What are you staring at?" Penn follows my gaze. "Oh. There's your future ball and chain."

"Mm."

"And her sister." Ari's tone sounds knowing. "Derek's stepdaughter. Aurora, wasn't it?"

I don't answer. Can't. Because Aurora just glanced up, her eyes sweeping across the club, and for one heartbeat, our gazes lock.

Her entire body goes rigid.

Then she tears her attention away, turning back to Olivia with forced brightness.

But I saw it. That flash of recognition. Of heat.

"Interesting," Ari murmurs.

I need to get her away from that table, away from Olivia. Somewhere we can talk without an audience and without my fiancée watching.

The question is how.

I drain my whiskey, eyes never leaving her. Even amid the club's manufactured glamour, Aurora radiates an authentic energy. She's trying not to look at me, but I catch the way her fingers tighten around her glass, the slight tension in her shoulders.

"I need to say hello to my fiancée," I announce, cutting off whatever Penn was saying.

Ari's eyebrow lifts. "Really? You've spent the entire night avoiding talking about her."

I give him a look that tells him to shut up if he wants to leave here breathing, and stand, straightening my cuffs as I move through the crowd. People part automatically. My focus narrows to that table, to Aurora's profile as she deliberately keeps her gaze averted from my approach.

She senses me coming. I can tell by the subtle shift of her body and the straightening of her spine. Fight or flight. But she'll do neither.

Olivia spots me first, her face lighting up with practiced perfection. "Hunter! What a surprise!"

Aurora goes completely still. The woman beside her glances between us with narrowed eyes.

"Ladies." I rest my hand on the back of the booth, directly behind Aurora. The heat of her body radiates against my arm. I could touch her if I shifted two inches. "I thought I should introduce myself to my fiancée's friends."

Olivia beams, making introductions, but I barely register. All my focus is on Aurora; on the slight tremble I detect when my fingers deliberately brush her shoulder as I extend my hand to the woman beside her.

When I finally look at Aurora directly, her eyes meet mine with defiance that does nothing to mask the chemistry between us. Challenge and heat and confusion all warring in those pretty blue depths.

"Aurora," I say, her name like a claim on my tongue. "Nice to see you again."

The table goes quiet. Her throat works as she swallows.

I nod. "Nice to see you too."

The challenge of extracting Aurora from her sister's watchful eye excites me. A predator never rushes, because patience is what ensures victory.

"Olivia, darling," I say, letting my hand rest possessively on her shoulder while my attention remains fixed on Aurora. "I need to borrow your sister for a moment."

Olivia blinks up at me, surprise flitting across her features. "What for?"

"I've been meaning to discuss the Harrison Foundation gala next month. Your father mentioned Aurora handles the family's charitable endeavors."

A perfect lie. Plausible and impossible for anyone at the table to verify immediately. Derek had mentioned no such thing, but my extensive research has given me the perfect ammunition.

"I didn't realize you were interested in the foundation," Olivia says, her smile faltering slightly.

"Reed Technologies is always looking for meaningful partnerships." I extend my hand to Aurora. "It won't take long."

Aurora hesitates, trapped. She can't refuse without raising questions. The dark-haired friend beside her is watching me as she can see straight through my bullshit, and she narrows her eyes.

"We were just celebrating your engagement," this friend says coolly.

"And you'll continue when I bring her back," I reply, not bothering to look away from Aurora. "Five minutes."

Aurora sets her glass down with deliberate care. "It's fine, Grace." She slides out from the booth, careful not to touch me. "The foundation is important."

I place my hand at the small of her back as I guide her away, feeling her body stiffen at my touch. The contact sends electricity through my palm. *Mine.* The thought blazes through me with primitive certainty.

I steer her toward the hallway leading to the private rooms Elixir reserves for VIPs—far enough from prying eyes but still within the club.

"There is no foundation discussion, is there?" Aurora says under her breath as we walk.

"No," I admit, applying the slightest pressure to guide her around a corner where we'll be completely hidden from view. "But we definitely need to talk."

I notice one of the private VIP rooms is empty and slip inside, closing the door behind us. The room is dimly lit with low, amber lights that cast shadows across her face, highlighting those defiant blue eyes.

"What do you want?" she asks, backing away.

I advance, maintaining the distance between us at exactly one step. Close enough to smell her light floral perfume, which makes my mouth water.

"You know exactly what I want." My voice comes out rougher than intended. "The same thing you want."

"I don't want anything from you." She tilts her chin up, but her pulse hammers visibly at the base of her throat. "Especially not now."

I move closer, watching her pupils dilate. "Liar."

The air between us crackles with sexual tension. I can almost taste it on my tongue.

"You're engaged to my sister." Her voice wavers slightly.

"A misunderstanding." I step closer, eliminating most of the space between us. "Nothing more."

"A misunderstanding?" she questions.

I tilt my head. "Yes, I approached your father to ask about a possible merger and wedding proposal, assuming you were Olivia Harrison, considering you were staying at Derek's home."

"That doesn't make this okay." Her breathing quickens, chest rising and falling rapidly.

I reach out, running my fingertips down her bare arm. Her skin pebbles under my touch, and she shivers but doesn't pull away.

"Tell me to stop," I challenge, moving my hand to her waist, my fingers splaying across the thin material of her dress. "Tell me you don't feel this."

She says nothing, her eyes locked on mine.

My body responds instantly to her proximity, my cock hardening painfully against my tailored pants. I step closer, letting her feel exactly what she does to me, pressing slightly against her.

Her breath catches.

"This isn't—" she starts, then stops when I raise my other hand to her face, tracing her cheekbone with my thumb.

"Isn't what?" I murmur, lowering my head until my lips hover just above hers. "Isn't right? Isn't what you thought about every night since the cliff?"

Her eyes flutter closed for a moment, and I can feel her resolve weakening. My entire body thrums with need, every nerve ending firing at once.

"Tell me you don't want this," I demand, my voice barely above a growl. The scent of jasmine and something uniquely Aurora floods my senses. My hand at her waist tightens. "Tell me you haven't thought about me every fucking night since we almost kissed."

Aurora's hands press against my chest, not quite pushing me away but creating distance. Her touch burns through my shirt.

"It doesn't matter what I want," she says, voice stronger than I expected. "You're engaged to my sister. I won't be the other woman, Hunter."

I step forward, eliminating the space she created. "An engagement that means nothing."

"It means something to Olivia." Her eyes flash with irritation even as her body betrays her, leaning infinitesimally toward mine. "I won't hurt her. I'm not that person."

"And I don't care." The truth spills out. "I'll break the engagement. I'll buy your father's company and dismantle it piece by piece. I'll burn down everything I've built." My hand slides to her throat, not squeezing, just feeling her pulse hammer against my palm. "I'll do whatever the fuck it takes to have you."

Her eyes widen, not with fear, but with recognition. She

sees me now. The real me. Not the polished businessman but the predator beneath.

And she's not running.

"You can't just take what you want," she whispers, but there's heat in her voice.

"I can. I do." I lean closer, my lips a breath from hers. "And I want you."

"You're insane." Her fingers curl into my shirt.

"Probably." My thumb traces her lower lip. "Does that scare you?"

Her pupils dilate, nearly swallowing the blue. "It should."

I can feel the dark attraction pulsing between us. She's drawn to the very parts of me others fear. The ruthlessness. The control.

"Say no," I challenge, my lips brushing the corner of her mouth. "Tell me to stop."

Her breathing quickens, her body arching toward mine. Instead of yielding, she turns her face at the last moment.

"No," she says, the word trembling between us. "Not like this. Not with Olivia in this same club."

I step closer, pinning her against the wall with my body. My hand slides from her throat to grip her jaw, forcing her to look at me.

"You want to know what I want?" My voice drops to a growl. "I want to tear that fucking dress off your body and bend you over right here. I want to spank that perfect ass until it's red and raw and you're begging me to stop."

Her breathing hitches, pupils blown wide with a mixture of fear and arousal.

"I want to fuck you until you scream my name," I continue, my words hot against her ear. "Until you forget your own. I want to mark every inch of your body so that everyone knows who you belong to."

My free hand grips her hip hard enough to bruise.

"I'd make you come on my tongue first, taste every inch of you. Then I'd fuck you rough and deep until you're ruined for any other man." I drag my teeth along the sensitive skin below her ear. "I want to see those pretty blue eyes water when you take me down your throat. I want to fill you up, claim you, own you."

I press my erection against her, letting her feel just how hard she makes me. "This is what you do to me. This is what I'm going to give you."

My fingers slide up her thigh, beneath the hem of her dress. "I'll take what's mine. And make no mistake, Aurora, you are mine."

She trembles against me, but then her hands flatten against my chest.

"Stop." Her voice cracks like a whip between us. "This isn't happening."

Her push catches me off guard, forcing me back half a step. Enough space for her to slip away from the wall.

"Whatever this is," she says, gesturing between us, her voice shaking, "it stops now. I won't betray my sister."

She straightens her dress with trembling fingers and backs toward the door.

"Stay away from me, Hunter."

She slams the door, leaving me alone with the ghost of her scent lingering in the air. The rejection isn't what I expected, but fuck if it doesn't make my cock throb harder in my pants.

My pulse thunders in my ears. The heat of her still burns on my palms.

This isn't over. Not by a fucking mile.

The way she stood up to me and those blue eyes flashed with both desire and determination, makes me harder than I've ever been. Most women fold under my gaze alone. Not Aurora. She pushes back. Challenges me.

I adjust myself, my erection straining painfully against my suit pants.

I never wanted someone with this level of intensity before. The fact that she walked away, that she's fighting this connection, only makes the hunt more exhilarating. She's prey worth pursuing.

Stay away from me, Hunter.

Her words echo in my mind, but they're not a deterrent. They're a gauntlet thrown down, a challenge I'm more than ready to accept. Her resistance has transformed desire into obsession.

I've never backed down from taking what I want. And I want Aurora Harrison more than I've ever wanted anything.

The higher the walls she builds, the more satisfaction I'll feel when I scale them and claim what's mine.

8

AURORA

The coffee splatters across my keyboard when I jolt awake from yet another Hunter Reed daydream. Perfect. Just perfect.

"Shit," I mutter, frantically dabbing tissues at my laptop. Three hours into my workday at Bloom's Press, and I've accomplished exactly nothing except ruining office equipment. This job offer is the main reason I left Europe.

My assistant editor, Mia, pokes her head in. "Everything okay in here? That's the second coffee casualty today."

"I'm fine. Just..." I gesture vaguely at the manuscript on my screen. "Really into this... werewolf romance?"

She raises an eyebrow. "The tax law handbook we're publishing next month?"

Fuck my life.

"Right. That's what I meant." I force a smile until she backs away, clearly unconvinced.

The moment she's gone, I drop my head onto my desk. This is pathetic. I'm pathetic. I've got my dream job running an entire publishing division, and I can't focus because my brain keeps replaying Hunter's hands on me, his voice in my ear, the way he said he wanted to—

Nope. Not going there. Not at work. Not ever.

I open my email, determined to be productive. Three sentences into a response about cover design options, and I'm back to remembering how he pinned me against that wall, how his breath felt against my neck, how—

"STOP IT," I say out loud, slapping my cheeks.

The intern walking past my office freezes like a startled rabbit.

"Not you!" I call after her retreating form. "Just talking to myself because I'm totally normal and professional!"

I glance at my phone, where Olivia's text from this morning still sits unanswered.

Wedding venue ideas? Thinking of the botanical gardens?

My stomach twists. My sister is planning her wedding to the man who told me in explicit detail how he wants to bend me over and—

I slam my laptop closed so hard the remaining coffee jumps from my mug onto my white blouse.

"Spectacular," I mutter, dabbing at the stain. "Truly spectacular performance today, Aurora."

My phone buzzes against my desk. I wipe my hands on a tissue and check the notification.

Unknown number: *Thinking about all those things I wanted to do to you?*

The coffee mug I'm holding nearly slips from my fingers. My pulse skyrockets.

Me: *Who is this?*

Unknown number: *You know exactly who this is, Aurora.*

Fuck. Hunter. How did he even get my number?

Me: *What do you want?*

Hunter: *I already told you that. In vivid detail, if I recall. Against a wall at Elixir.*

Heat floods my face. I glance around my office; suddenly paranoid someone could see my screen.

Me: *I'm working. Please leave me alone.*

Hunter: *Are you? Because from where I'm sitting, you've been staring into space for the last twenty minutes. Spilled coffee twice.*

My blood turns to ice. I snap my head up, scanning the windows of my office.

Me: *How the fuck do you know that?*

Hunter: *Look out your window, Aurora. The building across from you.*

I stand up so quickly my chair rolls back and hits the wall. I stride to my corner office windows and look up.

There he is. In the gleaming glass tower directly across from mine. Hunter Reed, standing at the window of what must be a corner office that perfectly mirrors mine, phone in hand, watching me like a hawk studying its prey.

He raises his hand in a small, mocking wave.

Me: *Are you fucking STALKING me now?*

Hunter: *Hardly stalking when it's my building. Reed Technologies. I own the entire block.*

Of course he does. Because the universe apparently wants me to suffer.

Hunter: *Nice blouse. White is your color.*

I slam my phone down on my desk and yank my blinds closed with such force I nearly tear them from the wall.

My phone buzzes again. I refuse to look at it for nearly a minute, but curiosity wins over pride.

Hunter: *You can shut me out with blinds, Aurora, but I'm not letting you go. Not now. Not ever.*

The intensity of his words sends an involuntary shiver through me. I type furiously.

Me: *You're ENGAGED to my SISTER. Do you understand what that means?*

Hunter: *Check your messages.*

The notification appears at the top of my screen. I tap it without thinking.

My breath catches in my throat. It's Hunter with his suit pants unbuttoned, expensive black boxers pushed down, his hand wrapped around...

Jesus Christ.

I slam my phone face-down on my desk, but it's too late. The image is seared into my brain. Hunter Reed is... proportional. Extremely proportional. The arrogant bastard has every right to be confident.

My thighs clench involuntarily. A wave of heat washes over me that has nothing to do with embarrassment and everything to do with something much more dangerous.

I grab my phone again.

Me: *You're being a fucking asshole to my sister. What is WRONG with you?*

Hunter: *Olivia and I aren't in love, Aurora. We've barely spoken three sentences to each other. It's an engagement of convenience that I could break any second.*

Me: *You can't just toy with people like this. She's planning a WEDDING.*

Hunter: *I don't want her. I want you. I've wanted you since I pulled you back from that cliff.*

My fingers hover over the keyboard. What do I even say to that? Every principle I have tells me to block his number, report him to HR, and tell my sister everything. But my body...my body is reacting in ways I can't control.

Hunter: *I can see you thinking, Aurora. Don't overthink this. We both want the same thing.*

I look up at my closed blinds, knowing he's over there with his cock hard, waiting for my response. Knowing he sent me that picture while looking directly at my office.

I stare at my phone screen, my heart hammering so hard I can feel it in my throat. Heat floods my body, pooling between my thighs, making me shift uncomfortably in my office chair. God, what is wrong with me? This is my sister's fiancé. This is wrong on so many levels.

But I can't stop thinking about that picture. About him. About what he's probably doing right now while looking at my office.

My fingers move before my brain can stop them.

Me: *Are you... touching yourself right now?*

The three dots appear immediately. He was waiting.

Hunter: *Yes. Thinking about you. Wishing it were your hand instead of mine.*

I press my thighs together, trying to quell the ache building there. This is ridiculous. I should be disgusted. I should be furious. Instead, I'm imagining walking across the street, taking the elevator up to his office, and—

Hunter: *Want to see? I can video call you.*

My breath catches. The rational part of my brain is screaming to shut this down now. Block his number. Tell Olivia everything. But my thumb hovers over the keyboard, trembling slightly.

Me: *I can't. We can't.*

Hunter: *We can do whatever we want, Aurora. No one has to know.*

I close my eyes, picturing Olivia's excited face this morning as she talked about flower arrangements. My sister. The only family I have left. The thought of her tears if she found out makes me feel sick.

But when I open my eyes again, I'm typing.

Me: *I want to. God help me, I want to. But Olivia...*

I delete the message before sending it and replace it with something shorter.

Me: *This needs to stop.*

But even as I type those words, I know I don't mean them. And worse—Hunter knows it too.

My phone lights up with another notification. Despite every warning bell in my head, I turn it over.

The photo nearly stops my heart. Hunter again, but this time his cock is fully erect, the tip glistening with pre-cum, his large hand wrapped around the shaft. The image is framed to show just enough of his expensive watch and suit pants pushed down to his thighs, somehow making it even more obscene.

"Oh..." A soft moan escapes my lips before I can stop it.

Heat rushes through my body, settling between my legs with such intensity that I press my thighs together. The pressure only makes it worse. Better. Whatever this is.

I glance up at my office door—still open. Anyone could walk by. Anyone could see me flushed and breathing hard over a dick pic from my sister's fiancé.

My legs feel unsteady as I stand, but I make it across the room. I close my office door with a decisive click.

Back at my desk, I stare at the photo again. My mouth has gone dry. I imagine how it would feel in my hand, against my lips, inside me—

God, what am I doing?

But the throbbing between my thighs doesn't care about morality or sisterhood or professionalism. My body has made its decision.

I sink into my chair, one hand mindlessly slipping to the waistband of my skirt as I type with the other.

Me: *You're going to destroy me.*

His response is immediate.

Hunter: *That's the plan, princess. Every fucking inch of you.*

My hands shake as I reach for my bag, fumbling for my Bluetooth earbuds. This is insane. I'm insane. But I can't stop.

"Fuck it," I whisper, slipping the earbuds in. I click the video call icon on Hunter's contact.

One ring. Two rings. My heart pounds so hard I feel lightheaded.

His face appears on screen, those beautiful eyes boring into mine. He's still in his office, jacket discarded, tie loosened. The ghost of a smirk plays on his lips.

"Look at you," he says, voice low and rough. "All flushed and bothered in your office."

"This is wrong," I whisper, but I don't hang up.

"Are you touching your pretty pussy like a good girl?" The crude words from his sophisticated mouth send a jolt straight between my legs.

I shake my head, embarrassed.

"Do it." It's not a request. "Show me."

My free hand slides under my skirt before I can talk myself out of it. I angle the phone down slightly, showing him as I push my panties aside. I'm already slick, embarrassingly wet.

"Fuck," he groans. "You're soaked for me."

The camera shifts as Hunter repositions his phone. He's fully exposed now, stroking himself slowly. The sight makes my mouth water.

"Touch yourself. Slow circles." His commanding tone brooks no argument.

I obey, gasping as my fingers slide through my wetness.

"Good girl," he praises, and the words send a rush of heat through me. "You're going to come for me while I watch."

"Hunter..." I whisper, knowing I shouldn't want this.

"Say it," he demands, his hand moving faster. "Say you're my good girl."

"I'm your good girl," I breathe, circling my clit faster.

"You belong to me, Aurora. Not anyone else. Mine." His breathing grows ragged as he strokes himself. "Show me how pretty you look when you come."

My hips buck against my hand as I feel the pressure building. This is madness. Complete madness.

But I can't stop now.

His face on my screen transforms, a feral intensity taking over his features as he watches me touch myself.

"You think this is wrong?" Hunter's voice drops impossibly lower, each word dripping with dark promise. "I'm just getting started with you. I'm going to make you crave things you've never even imagined."

My fingers move faster, my body betraying every moral principle I've ever had.

"Look at you, so desperate in your perfect little office. I'm going to break you apart, Aurora. Not just your body, but your mind." His breathing grows harsher. "I'm going to ruin you for anyone else. You'll feel me everywhere, in everything you do."

"Hunter, please..." I whimper, not even knowing what I'm begging for.

"I can see it in your eyes, that fear mixed with want. That's what gets me hard. Knowing I could destroy everything you care about, and you'd still spread your legs for me." His hand moves faster. "You want to be good, but you're dripping wet for the man who's going to ruin you."

His words shouldn't affect me, but they do. They slice through my defenses, each syllable pushing me closer to the edge.

"When I finally get inside you, I'm going to watch you break apart on my cock. Watch that perfect facade crumble. I want to see the moment you realize you've given everything to me; Your body, your loyalty, your fucking soul."

The pressure builds impossibly as his voice goes razor-sharp.

"Come for me now. Show me what I own."

My body convulses violently, a scream catching in my throat as waves of pleasure crash through me. I've never come this hard as my body arches off the chair and warm liquid gushes between my thighs, soaking my hand.

"Fuck," Hunter growls, his own control shattering as he watches me. "You're fucking perfect when you come." His muscles tense, jaw clenching as he comes in thick ropes across his stomach, never breaking eye contact.

For several heartbeats, there's nothing but our ragged breathing in the silence.

"Oh my god," I gasp, reality crashing down on me as the pleasure subsides. "This didn't happen. This absolutely did not happen."

My hand is still between my legs, evidence of my betrayal wet against my fingers. Hunter's face on my screen shows a satisfied smirk that makes my stomach turn.

"Never text me again," I stammer, voice trembling with shock at what I've just done. "Never call me again. This was a mistake. A horrible mistake."

Before he can respond, I end the call with shaking

fingers and throw my phone onto my desk like it's burned me.

"What have I done?" I whisper to the empty office, tears springing to my eyes.

I look down at my rumpled skirt, the wet patch on my chair. Shame floods through me, hot and suffocating. I just got myself off on camera for my sister's fiancé. In my office. In the middle of a workday.

I grab tissues from my desk drawer, frantically wiping between my legs, cleaning the chair, trying to erase the evidence of my weakness. But no amount of cleaning can wash away what I've done to Olivia.

My phone buzzes against my desk. I know who it is before I even look.

Hunter: *You can try to run from this, Aurora. You can pretend it didn't happen. You can block my number. But there's nowhere on this earth you could go to escape me.*

I stare at the message, a cold shiver running down my spine. It should read as a threat. Instead, some twisted part of me thrills at his words.

And that terrifies me more than anything.

9

HUNTER

My reflection stares back at me in the tinted window of the Bentley as we glide through downtown traffic. There's something different in my eyes now. A hunger I've never experienced before.

Aurora Harrison. The image of her coming undone on my screen replays in my mind—lips parted, that perfect moment when she surrendered completely. Mine. The word echoes inside my skull with each heartbeat.

I adjust myself in the leather seat, still hard at just the memory. This isn't like the usual conquests, the faceless women who warm my bed then disappear before morning. This is something else entirely.

"Sir, we'll arrive at the meeting in approximately eight minutes," my driver announces through the intercom.

I don't respond. My mind is elsewhere. In her office, watching her fingers work between her thighs while I commanded her pleasure from across the street. The power of it was intoxicating.

I pull out my phone, scroll through our messages, and

pause at the image I sent her. Calculated risk. I knew she wouldn't be able to resist.

Her final message attempts defiance as if she could cut me out now, after what we've shared. Impossible.

"I'll break you," I whisper to her image on my screen. "Every resistance, every hesitation, every thought of your sister. I'll burn it all away until there's nothing left but your need for me."

This isn't just desire. It's ownership. Possession. I've built empires, destroyed competitors, amassed more wealth than most countries, but nothing has ever felt like this obsessive need to claim every part of her.

The engagement to Olivia is a temporary inconvenience. A business arrangement that can be dissolved easily when the time comes. Aurora is different. The challenge of taking what isn't freely given, of conquering that fire in her eyes, consumes me.

Breaking my engagement with Olivia will require finesse. The Harrison contracts are too valuable to jeopardize with a messy split. I need to create distance first and arrange for Olivia to discover compromising photos. A woman in my bed, carefully selected not to resemble Aurora. The tabloids would eat it alive, and Olivia's pride would force her to end things publicly.

I check my watch. Three days. That's all I need to implement this plan and be free to claim what's mine.

"Sir, we've arrived," Daniels announces, pulling the Bentley to a stop outside the abandoned warehouse that serves as our Selection headquarters.

I exit without acknowledging him. The building's exterior is crumbling brick and rusted metal, which belies what lies within. Inside, fifteen candidates stand in a neat row, backs straight, eyes forward. Each one vetted thoroughly, their backgrounds dissected, their weaknesses cataloged.

Ari, Penn, Blaine, and Grayson await me on a raised platform. I take my position at the center, surveying the nervous faces below.

"Congratulations on reaching this stage," I begin, voice carrying easily through the cavernous space. "Currently, you believe this is an opportunity. By tomorrow, half of you will understand it's a nightmare."

I pace slowly before them, studying each face. "Five of you will become Vipers. The rest will suffer consequences for wasting our time."

A young man in the front row swallows visibly. I stop directly in front of him.

"Something to say?" I ask softly.

"No, sir."

I smile. "Your file says you have a wife. Two children. How far would you go to protect them?"

He pales. "Whatever it takes."

"We'll see." I continue down the line. "The tests you face will strip away your humanity piece by piece. We need to know what remains when everything else is gone."

I turn to address them all. "Those with true potential understand that morality is a luxury for the weak. Power belongs to those willing to do whatever is necessary."

"Strip," I command, my voice echoing through the warehouse. "Everything except boxers."

The candidates exchange nervous glances before complying. Clothes drop to the floor, revealing varying physiques from sculpted to soft. Vulnerability makes them shift uncomfortably under our scrutiny.

"Pathetic," Penn mutters beside me, examining the lineup with predatory eyes.

I press a button, and metal tables rise from beneath the floor, each bearing identical wooden boxes.

"Open them," I order.

Fifteen lids lift simultaneously. Inside each box: a serrated hunting knife and a photograph.

"The person in your photograph is currently held in our facility," I explain, watching their faces contort with confusion. "Some are criminals. Some are innocents. You don't get to know which."

I pause, letting the implication settle.

"Your first task is simple. You will extract information from your subject. We want to know the location of a digital file. Use whatever methods necessary."

Grayson steps forward, his voice clinical. "Half of your subjects know nothing. They're merely here to test your... discernment."

A muscular candidate raises his hand. "What if they don't know anything?"

I smile. "Then you'd better hope you discover that before you waste too much time. Because the last three to retrieve the correct information are eliminated."

"And if we refuse?" asks another, the executive with the family.

Ari laughs, the sound sharp in the concrete space. "Then you forfeit. Along with everyone connected to you."

I nod toward the far wall. It slides open to reveal fifteen bloodied figures already strapped to metal chairs.

"Begin."

The candidates approach their assigned victims. Some hesitate, knuckles white around their knife handles. Others move with disturbing eagerness.

Blood spatters across pale skin as the first cut is made. A

scream rips through the air, followed by desperate pleading.

"He's innocent! He knows nothing!" one candidate shouts, backing away from his sobbing subject.

I check my watch. "That's your assessment? You're certain?"

"Yes."

"Wrong." I press another button, flooding his station with electric current.

Both candidate and subject convulse in synchronized agony before collapsing.

"Fourteen remaining," I announce. "I suggest you work faster."

I lean against the railing, savoring the metallic scent of fear and blood that permeates the air. There's a unique satisfaction in watching desperation transform people, stripping away their pretenses of morality until nothing remains but their true nature. Some break immediately. Others fight it. The resistance is what makes this entertaining.

The executive with the family catches my eye. Tears stream down his face as he presses the blade against his subject's forearm. His hand trembles, weakness incarnate.

"Deeper," I call out, my voice echoing through the warehouse. "She can't feel it unless you mean it."

His eyes meet mine, pleading for mercy I don't possess. I raise an eyebrow, and he complies, pressing until crimson wells around stainless steel. The woman screams. Music to my ears.

How fascinating, watching someone destroy themselves to save themselves. The paradox never gets old.

"Fifteen minutes remaining," I announce, checking my

watch unnecessarily. The announcement is merely to increase their panic.

Penn sidles up beside me. "Number eight looks promising."

I follow his gaze to a woman working, her face devoid of emotion as she carves patterns into her sobbing subject's chest. She hasn't asked a single question yet, causing pain for its own sake. Intriguing.

"Note that one," I murmur. "She understands the real purpose."

Because this isn't about information, it's about seeing who can become the monster we need them to be.

I feel nothing as I watch these strangers suffer. Their pain exists solely for my entertainment and evaluation. Their lives are mine to redirect or destroy, pieces on my board.

A man collapses, vomiting onto the concrete after cutting too deep. Pathetic. I signal to Grayson, who efficiently removes the failure and his still-screaming victim.

"Thirteen," I announce, enjoying how the single word sends fresh panic through the remaining candidates.

My phone vibrates in my pocket. A message from Aurora.

You're insane. Stay away from me.

I smile. Her resistance only heightens my determination. I type a response, deliberate with each word.

You came for me. I watched you surrender. We both know what you want.

I slip my phone away, returning my attention to the bloodied warehouse floor. Three candidates have retrieved the correct information, standing apart from the others with vacant expressions. It's the first sign they're becoming what we need.

Number eight, the woman Penn noticed, approaches her subject without hesitation. She's extracted nothing but has inflicted extraordinary pain. When she finally asks her first question, the subject immediately gives up the location. Interesting technique—pure terror before interrogation.

"Time," I announce, causing panicked movements from those still working. "Step away from your subjects."

As the candidates form a line, I walk before them, studying faces streaked with blood and sweat. My phone buzzes again, but I ignore it. Aurora can wait.

I study the remaining thirteen candidates; blood splattered across their skin like modern art. Some stand tall with cold detachment in their eyes—potential. Others tremble, unable to meet my gaze.

"Candidates three and seven, step forward."

They move with hesitation, fear evident in every step. Candidate three still clutches his knife, knuckles white. Seven's hands shake uncontrollably, tears streaming down his face.

"You were the slowest to extract information," I state, voice devoid of emotion. "More importantly, you showed reluctance when faced with necessity."

"Please," Seven whispers. "I have a family."

I smile. "You should have considered them before wasting our time."

Penn approaches with swift efficiency, placing a gun in my outstretched hand. The metal feels cool against my palm, an extension of my will. I raise it without hesitation.

"Wait—" Three begins.

The shot echoes through the warehouse. Three crumples to the floor, a perfect hole between his eyes. Seven falls to his knees, sobbing.

"Take him to processing," I tell Grayson. "Make sure he understands the consequences of failure."

Grayson nods, dragging the broken man away. His screams fade as they disappear through the metal door.

I turn to the eleven surviving candidates. "Congratulations on passing the first test. Clean yourselves up and prepare for tomorrow."

As they file out, I check my phone. Three messages from Aurora, each more desperate than the last.

You can't do this. I won't let you.

I'll tell Olivia everything.

Hunter, please. Don't make me destroy us both.

A smile curves my lips. I tuck the phone away and step over the cooling body on the concrete floor.

The selection continues tomorrow. For now, I have a different target to pursue.

10

AURORA

I stare at my reflection in the bathroom mirror, toothbrush frozen midair. Dark circles shadow my eyes after a night spent tossing and turning, my mind in an endless loop of yesterday's virtual encounter with Hunter.

What have I done?

My stomach twists as I rinse my mouth, unable to wash away the sour taste of self-disgust. I close my eyes but see only Hunter's face, hear his commands, feel the phantom touch of hands that were never actually on my body.

And Olivia... sweet, trusting Olivia.

I splash cold water on my face, hoping it might shock away the guilt that clings to me like a second skin. It doesn't.

The kitchen smells of fresh coffee and cinnamon when I trudge downstairs. Olivia dances around the island in silk pajamas, hair piled messily atop her head, humming while she arranges pastries on a plate.

"Morning, sleepyhead!" She beams, sliding a steaming mug toward me. "You look terrible. Rough night?"

I force myself to meet her eyes. "Just couldn't sleep."

"Well, this will perk you up." She pushes an ornate envelope across the counter. "Look what arrived this morning!"

My fingers tremble as I open it, revealing an invitation printed on heavy black card stock with silver embossing.

"The Vipers' annual masquerade ball," Olivia squeals, clutching my arm. "Hunter's friends throw the most exclusive party in the city. Nobody gets in without a personal invitation."

The silver text glimmers mockingly: *The pleasure of your company is requested at the 15th Annual Masquerade Ball. Masks mandatory. Secrets optional.*

"Hunter added your name to our invitation," Olivia continues, oblivious to my growing nausea. "Isn't that thoughtful? Now you can help me shop for the perfect dress and mask!"

The mug slips from my grasp, hot coffee splashing across the counter. "Sorry," I mumble, frantically mopping up the mess while avoiding her gaze.

"You okay? You've been acting weird."

"Just tired," I lie, my voice strangled. "The masquerade sounds... interesting."

"Interesting? It's legendary! And now you'll be there with me, with us." She hugs me from behind, her chin resting on my shoulder.

Each word is another twist of the knife I've plunged into her back.

"I should get to work." I grab my purse, desperate to escape before my face betrays me. "Deadline for the feature article is tomorrow."

Olivia wipes her hands on a kitchen towel. "Sure. Will

we talk wedding details over dinner? I'm thinking blush pink for the bridesmaids."

The word "wedding" hits like a physical blow. "Sounds perfect." My smile feels brittle enough to crack my face.

"Love you, sis!" Olivia calls as I practically sprint to the door.

"Love you too." The words taste like ash.

In my car, I grip the steering wheel until my knuckles turn white. The image of Olivia's trusting face collides with memories of what Hunter and I did yesterday. My stomach churns.

I slam my palm against the wheel. "What is wrong with me?"

Traffic crawls on the expressway, trapping me with my thoughts. I switch on the radio, cranking the volume until the bass drowns out the voice in my head listing all the ways I've betrayed my sister.

My phone buzzes. Hunter. I ignore it.

It buzzes again. And again.

At a red light, I glance down.

Hunter: *Morning, Aurora. Still thinking about yesterday.*

Hunter: *I can't focus. All I see is you.*

Hunter: *You can ignore me, but we both know what happened.*

I throw the phone onto the passenger seat like it's burning my fingers. The light turns green, and I press the accelerator too hard.

By the time I reach Bloom's Press, three more messages have arrived. I don't read them.

"Morning, sunshine!" My coworker Grace waves from her desk. "You look like death warmed over."

"Thanks," I mutter, ducking into my office and closing the door.

My phone buzzes again. Hunter sent a photo. I delete it without opening it, hands shaking.

I stare at my computer screen, trying to focus on the article about urban renewal. The words blur together. My phone lights up. Again. Again.

"Stop," I whisper, turning the phone face down.

I type three sentences, delete two. The blinking cursor mocks me. My phone vibrates against the desk, inching forward with each message.

Ten new texts by lunch. All ignored. I can't block him because I know he'd find a way around it. But I can't answer him either.

I'm trapped, suffocating under the weight of a mistake that keeps growing with every message I refuse to read.

A tap on my door interrupts my spiral of guilt and panic.

"Ms. Harrison?" My assistant Zoe peeks in, her expression apologetic. "There's a call for you on line one. The gentleman says it's urgent."

I rub my temples, grateful for the distraction from Hunter's barrage of texts. "Did they give a name?"

"Um, he said you'd want to take it." Zoe shifts uncomfortably. "Something about a Harrison Foundation matter?"

My stomach drops. Only one person would use that excuse.

"Thanks, Zoe. I'll take it."

After she closes the door, I stare at the blinking phone light. One, two, three breaths. I pick up.

"This is Aurora Harrison."

"You've been ignoring my messages."

Hunter's voice slides through the receiver like warm honey, making my skin prickle with unwanted awareness.

"I'm working." I glance at my office door, lowering my voice. "Don't call me here again."

"You left me no choice, Aurora."

"We have nothing to discuss." My fingers tighten around the phone. "What happened was a mistake. It's over."

His low chuckle makes my stomach flip. "Nothing between us is over."

"Goodbye, Hunter."

I move to slam down the receiver, my hand trembling with anger and something else I refuse to name.

"Hang up, and I'll call Olivia next."

I freeze, the phone hovering above its cradle.

"What did you say?" My voice is barely audible.

"I'm calling from my office. One button, and I'm connected to my fiancée." The way he says 'fiancée' drips with mockery. "I wonder how she'd feel about our little video session yesterday? Finding out her sister touched herself while watching me?"

Cold dread washes through me. "You wouldn't."

"Talk to me, or find out." His voice hardens. "Your choice, Aurora."

I sink back into my chair, trapped. "What do you want?" I ask, my voice barely more than a whisper.

"You." The single word hangs between us, charged and dangerous. "I want you, Aurora. Tonight."

My throat tightens. "That's not happening."

"I need to see you in the flesh. Somewhere private." His voice drops lower, that same commanding tone that made me do things I never thought I would. "No screens between us this time."

I press my fingertips against my temple, trying to quell the panic rising in my chest. "No. Absolutely not."

"This isn't a request."

"I don't care what you call it," I snap, anger momentarily overtaking fear. "I'm not meeting you."

"Your sister doesn't have to know about us."

"There is no us, Hunter." I glance at my office door, paranoid someone might overhear. "What happened was a mistake. One I won't repeat."

His laugh is soft, menacing. "We both know that's a lie. I saw your face, Aurora. I heard the sounds you made."

Heat floods my cheeks. "Stop."

"Meet me tonight. My place. Ten o'clock."

"No." I dig my nails into my palm. "I won't betray my sister again."

"Such loyalty." His tone shifts, harder now. "Fine. If you won't come to me, I'll come to you."

My heart stutters. "What?"

"I've been invited to have dinner with Derek tonight to discuss wedding arrangements. I planned on saying I had other plans. But I'll be at the estate, Aurora." The threat in his voice is unmistakable. "I'll find a way to be alone with you."

"Don't you dare," I whisper, panic clawing up my throat.

"Watch me." His voice drops to a predatory purr. "I always get what I want, Aurora. Always. And right now, what I want is you. Ten o'clock. The garden. Or I make my own opportunity."

"Hunter—"

The line goes dead. I sigh, dropping the phone as if it's burned me. My head falls into my hands, but I can't ignore the heat spreading through my body. Just his demanding and confident voice has left me undeniably aroused. My thighs press together involuntarily, seeking pressure against the ache building there.

"What is wrong with me?" I whisper to my empty office. This man is blackmailing me, threatening to tell my sister, and yet my body responds like he's offering salvation instead of damnation.

My phone buzzes with a text notification. For a moment, I think it's Hunter again, but Daisy's name flashes on the screen instead.

Daisy: *Has Olivia heard about what happened with Hunter yet? It's been almost a week, Aurora.*

My stomach twists with fresh guilt. Grace must have told her about my promise to confess. I type and delete three different responses before settling on honesty.

Me: *No. I keep trying to find the right moment, but there isn't one. How do I tell my sister I'm lusting after her fiancé?*

Daisy: *You need to tell her before she finds out another way. That would be so much worse.*

Me: *I know. I will. Soon.*

I set the phone down, the weight of Daisy's concern adding to my already crushing guilt. She's right. I need to tell Olivia before Hunter does something that exposes us. Before tonight. Before ten o'clock in the garden.

But the thought of facing my sister, of watching her face crumple when she realizes what I've done... It's almost unbearable.

Almost as unbearable as the thought of meeting Hunter tonight, knowing what will happen if we're alone together again.

11

HUNTER

I straighten my tie as I approach the Harrison mansion, my mind already skipping ahead to what comes after this tedious dinner. Ten o'clock. The garden. Aurora.

Derek's butler greets me at the door with his usual stiff formality. "Mr. Reed, welcome. Mr. Harrison is waiting for you in the dining room."

I nod, handing off my coat. "Is the whole family joining us tonight?"

"Just Mr. Harrison, sir. Miss Olivia is attending a charity function, and Miss Aurora mentioned having work to catch up on in her room."

Perfect. My lips twitch with satisfaction. Aurora is hiding.

The dining room doors open to reveal Derek already seated at the head of the table, a crystal tumbler of whiskey in hand. He stands when he sees me, his movements already slightly sluggish. Two drinks in, at least.

"Hunter! Right on time." He gestures to the chair at his right. "Sit, sit. We have business to discuss."

I force a smile as I take my seat. "Derek."

A server appears immediately with a matching tumbler of whiskey for me. Another advantage—Derek rarely conducts business without alcohol, making my abstinence easy to disguise. I'll need my wits about me tonight.

"I've been looking at the potential merger benefits," Derek says, unfolding a portfolio of documents. "The numbers look promising."

While he drones on, I check my watch discreetly. 7:30. Two and a half hours until Aurora. I can practically feel her presence somewhere above us in the house, probably pacing her room, debating whether to meet me.

She will. The alternative is far worse for her.

"Something pressing this evening, Hunter?" Derek catches my glance at the watch.

"Not at all. Just confirming we have plenty of time." I gesture toward his whiskey. "I know you prefer to wrap things up by ten."

He chuckles. "You know me well. Never could see the point of business talk past drinking hours."

Another server enters with the first course, and I settle in for the performance ahead. Derek will be five or six drinks in by nine-thirty, making my exit through the garden completely unremarkable.

The next two and a half hours unfold exactly as I predict. Derek Harrison, for all his business acumen, is utterly predictable when it comes to social routines.

During the first courses, it's pure market projections and acquisition talk. Derek gestures broadly with his fork, nearly toppling his second whiskey. "The Harrison-Reed merger will reshape the entire tech landscape." The same phrase he's used in our last three meetings.

I nod at appropriate intervals, offering calculated

responses while my mind drifts upstairs to Aurora. Is she watching the clock as intensely as I am?

Over the next course, we dive into Derek's complaints about the board. "Those fossils wouldn't recognize innovation if it bit them in the ass." His standard line, delivered as the salmon arrives. I've heard this speech so many times I could recite it verbatim.

And by the third course, Derek transitions to personal territory, right on schedule. Three more whiskeys in, his words slur slightly around the edges. "Olivia's thrilled about the engagement. Always knew she'd make a strategic match."

I check my watch. 9:05.

"The thing about my Olivia," Derek continues, pouring himself another drink without offering me one —he stopped noticing I wasn't drinking an hour ago— "is she understands what builds legacy. Not like Aurora. Too much of her mother in her. Impulsive. Emotional."

My fingers tighten around my fork hearing anyone speak badly of her. Derek doesn't notice.

The dessert arrives at 9:27. Derek's speech has devolved into his usual philosophical ramblings about wealth and power. I've heard this monologue at least five times before, each word as unoriginal as the last.

"Money isn't everything, Hunter," he says, despite his entire life suggesting otherwise. "It's the only thing." He laughs at his own joke—the same one he tells at every dinner.

I check my watch again. 9:41.

Derek yawns, right on cue. "Should probably call it a night. Early meeting tomorrow."

Predictable to the last second.

"I should be going as well." I stand, straightening my jacket. "Don't worry about seeing me out. I know the way."

Derek waves a dismissive hand, eyes already heavy with whiskey. "Good man. We'll continue this conversation next week."

"Looking forward to it." The lie slides easily from my lips.

I walk slowly through the grand hallway, nodding at a maid who scurries past. Only when I hear Derek's study door close behind him do I change direction. Instead of heading toward the front door, I turn down the corridor leading to the east wing.

The Harrison estate is mapped perfectly in my mind—I memorized the layout weeks ago. The garden entrance is accessible through a set of French doors off the solarium. As I pass through the dimly lit room, moonlight spills across marble floors, casting long shadows.

Nine fifty. Ten minutes early.

I step outside, the cool night air a welcome change from the stuffy formality inside. Derek's garden is immaculate—geometric hedges and stone pathways illuminated by subtle landscape lighting. I position myself beneath an ancient oak tree where shadows conceal my presence but allow me a clear view of the house.

From here, I can observe all potential approaches Aurora might take. Will she sneak out through the kitchen? The side door? Or boldly walk out through the solarium as I did?

I check my watch. Nine fifty-two.

Patience has always come naturally to me. In business, I've waited years for the perfect moment to acquire failing companies. I've outlasted opponents in negotiations until they cracked from the pressure of silence.

For Aurora, I would wait much longer.

Perhaps she's debating whether to come at all. The thought nearly makes me smile. Her reluctance is merely an inconvenience, not an obstacle. Whether she realizes it or not, our collision course was set the moment I pulled her back from that cliff edge.

Nine fifty-six.

I adjust my position slightly, remaining in the shadows.

Nine fifty-nine.

Movement catches my eye. A silhouette slips through the solarium doors—Aurora. One minute early.

Something primal stirs in my chest. She came. Despite her protests, her guilt, her sister—she's here. The knowledge settles into my bones with a deep, visceral satisfaction. I remain motionless in the shadows, watching her.

She steps hesitantly onto the stone path, moonlight catching in her dark hair. Her eyes dart around the garden, searching. Nervous. She's wearing a simple black sweater and jeans—attempting to blend into the night. How adorable.

Aurora takes another step forward, arms wrapped protectively around herself. She hasn't spotted me yet. The power of observation without being observed sends a rush of pleasure through my veins. This is the moment before the strike, the perfect stillness before conquest.

"Hunter?" she whispers, voice barely audible above the gentle rustle of leaves.

I don't answer immediately. Instead, I savor the way her eyes dart around nervously, searching for me. She takes another step forward, and I can see her pulse fluttering at her throat like a trapped bird.

"I know you're here," she says, stronger this time. "Let's just get this over with."

She's still fighting, still pretending she has a choice in this. That she doesn't want it as much as I do.

Her resistance is the most exquisite part. Any woman would come running at my command, except Aurora. She fights her desire even as she submits to it. She hates herself for wanting me, yet here she stands, one minute early.

I step out from the shadows, my movement deliberate and silent. When she finally sees me, her sharp intake of breath is audible. Her pupils dilate instantly.

"You came," I say, voice low.

Aurora's chin lifts slightly. "You didn't give me much choice."

I move toward her, close enough to catch her scent—something floral. "We both know that's not entirely true."

Her pulse quickens visibly at her throat as I step closer. Each heartbeat betraying what her words attempt to deny.

"I shouldn't be here," Aurora whispers, but she doesn't back away.

"Yet here you are." I reach out, trailing a finger along her jawline. She flinches but doesn't pull away. "One minute early, in fact."

"To tell you this has to stop." Her voice wavers unconvincingly.

I smile, circling behind her. She remains frozen as I lean in, my lips grazing her ear. "Your mouth says one thing, but your body..." I place my hands on her hips, pulling her back against me. "Your body tells a different story."

"Hunter..." Her protest dissolves into a soft gasp as I slide one hand up her ribcage, stopping just beneath her breast.

"Tell me to stop," I challenge, my thumb tracing slow circles on her side. "Say the words like you mean them."

She trembles against me but remains silent. I turn her

to face me, backing her against the ancient oak tree. Moonlight cuts across her features, illuminating the war playing out in her eyes—desire fighting desperately against loyalty.

"This is wrong," she manages, even as her hands reach for my shoulders.

"Then why does it feel inevitable?" I press my body against hers, pinning her to the tree. When my thigh slides between her legs, her sharp intake of breath is victory enough.

I capture her mouth with mine, swallowing her resistance. For three heartbeats, she remains rigid before surrendering with a whimper that vibrates through my chest. Her fingers thread through my hair, pulling me closer as her hips rock instinctively against my thigh.

The kiss deepens, turns savage. I taste her desperation, her guilt, her need—all of it fueling my own. My hand finds her breast, thumb circling her hardened nipple through the thin fabric of her sweater. She moans into my mouth, arching against my palm.

"This doesn't mean anything," she gasps when we break for air, even as her body contradicts every word.

I laugh softly against her neck. "Lie to yourself if you must, Aurora. But don't lie to me."

Her body trembles against mine, betraying every denial her lips attempt. I press harder against her, pushing her into the rough bark of the oak tree. The moonlight catches in her eyes—defiance and desire battling for dominance.

"Stop fighting this," I whisper against her throat, teeth grazing the sensitive skin where her pulse hammers wildly. "Stop fighting me."

"I hate you," Aurora breathes, but her hands contradict her words as they slide beneath my jacket, nails digging into my back.

"No, you don't." I capture her wrists, pinning them above her head with one hand. "You hate that you want me."

With my free hand, I trace the curve of her hip, slowly inching her sweater upward, revealing a strip of pale skin. The cool night air raises goosebumps across her stomach. I brush my fingers along the edge of her jeans, feeling her abdominal muscles contract under my touch.

"Hunter..." Her voice is barely audible, half warning, half plea.

I press my thigh harder between her legs, feeling her heat against me. The friction draws a gasp from her lips that shoots straight to my groin. I want to devour the sound, so I claim her mouth again, swallowing her moan.

Her resistance melts with each passing second. When I release her wrists, her hands immediately tangle in my hair, pulling me closer with unexpected force. The aggression surprises me. I growl against her mouth, my hands finding the bare skin of her waist, fingers digging into her flesh.

"Tell me you want this," I demand, breaking the kiss to look into her eyes. "Say it."

Aurora's chest rises and falls rapidly, her lips swollen from our kisses. "I shouldn't..."

"That's not what I asked." I slide my hand higher under her sweater, tracing the underside of her breast over her bra. "Tell me you want me."

She arches into my touch involuntarily. "Yes," she whispers, eyes closing in surrender. "God help me, yes."

I reach for the button of her jeans, my fingers working the metal disc free when—

A security light flashes on near the kitchen entrance. Through the windows, shadows move inside the house. Aurora freezes against me, her eyes widening in panic.

"Someone's coming," she hisses, pushing at my chest.

I remain pressed against her.

"This isn't over," I promise.

Aurora's eyes flash with something between fear and defiance. She pushes against my chest harder, creating distance between us.

"No, Hunter. It is over." Her voice trembles but firms with each word. "It has to be."

I reach for her wrist, but she steps backward, evading my grasp. The security light casts harsh shadows across her face, highlighting the conflict in her eyes.

"You don't mean that," I say. I know what I felt in her response to me. Her body doesn't lie, even when her mouth does.

"I do mean it." She wraps her arms around herself, as if physically holding herself together. "This was a mistake. All of it."

I take a step toward her. She counters with another step back.

"You need to stay away from me," Aurora says, her eyes darting toward the house again. "And I need to stay away from you."

"We both know that's not possible."

She shakes her head, a strand of dark hair falling across her face. "It has to be. You're engaged to my sister."

"An arrangement that means nothing."

"It means something to her." Her voice cracks slightly. "And she means everything to me."

I study her face, noting the way her pulse still races at her throat, how her pupils remain dilated despite her protests.

"You can say whatever you want, Aurora, but we both know the truth."

"The truth is you need to stay away from me." Her voice hardens with determination. "This ends now."

Before I can respond, she turns and runs toward the house, moving quickly along the stone path. I watch her retreat, noting the slight stumble in her step, the way her hand briefly touches the wall for support as she reaches the solarium doors.

I remain motionless in the shadows, watching as she slips back inside the house. The door closes behind her with a soft click that carries across the silent garden.

I smile to myself. Her words mean nothing. Her resistance only sharpens my resolve.

No one runs from me.

12

HUNTER

I study the monitor displaying the trembling man in my basement. Sweat gleams on his forehead as he stares at the box I've placed before him. Nine candidates left. Six eliminated. The weak ones break early.

"Please," he whispers, voice cracking. "I can't do this."

I press the intercom button. "You have two minutes to open the box, Mr. Sullivan." My voice echoes through the soundproofed room. Clinical. Detached. "Or you're eliminated."

Penn stands beside me, analyzing Sullivan's microexpressions. "He'll fold."

"Agreed." I check my watch. "Disappointing."

The candidate's hands shake as he reaches for the box, then withdraws. His eyes dart to the camera, desperate for mercy. He won't find any here. The Vipers don't accept weakness.

I lean closer to the microphone. "Ninety seconds."

"What's in it?" Sullivan's voice breaks. "Just tell me what's inside."

I smile. "The box contains your future. Or the end of it."

On the adjacent screens, I monitor the other tests. Ari's social manipulation challenge has already eliminated three candidates who couldn't maintain their cover stories under pressure. Blaine broke two more during the physical endurance test. Grayson's criminal operation simulation exposed another who balked at crossing certain lines.

Sullivan finally lifts the lid with trembling fingers.

His scream is satisfying. Pure terror. The kind that strips men bare.

"Please!" He scrambles backward. "Get it away from me!"

I check his file again. Severe arachnophobia. Noted during the preliminary psychological assessment.

"Remove it from the box before the timer ends, Mr. Sullivan."

"I can't! Please!"

"Then you're not Viper material." I press the button that releases the door. "Exits open. You're dismissed."

He bolts, leaving the box behind.

Penn marks something on his tablet. "Eight left."

I nod, already reviewing the next candidate's file. "Bring in Hansen. His fear is different. More... interesting."

"You're enjoying this." Penn's observation isn't a question.

I don't deny it. Breaking people reveals their core, showing what they're truly made of. Most are disappointingly fragile.

"We will send the remaining seven to my estate out of town tomorrow night if the next one passes. Final phase. I want to see which ones survive the breaking point. I am not confident that we will have five candidates standing in the end."

Penn watches Sullivan flee down the hall, then turns to

me with that irritating smirk. "Seven candidates, five spots. Not great odds." He leans against the control panel, deliberately casual. "Speaking of odds stacked against you—gotten over that Harrison girl yet? Or have you finally accepted your fate as Olivia's dutiful husband?"

I fix him with a cold stare. "When have I ever accepted anything less than exactly what I want?"

"Ah, yes. The great Hunter Reed, master of the universe." Penn's laugh echoes through the monitoring room. "Even you can't always get what you want, Hunt. Some things are... complicated."

"Complicated?" I adjust the camera angle to prepare for the next candidate. "That's a word people use when they lack the resolve to solve problems."

"And being engaged to the sister of the woman you're obsessed with isn't a problem?"

"It's a temporary inconvenience."

Penn shakes his head. "You're fucking insane, you know that? Most men would consider engagement a rather permanent inconvenience."

"Most men aren't me." I check my watch, deliberately changing the subject. "Hansen will be here in five minutes."

Penn pushes off from the panel. "So what's the plan? Marry Olivia, fuck Aurora on the side, and hope daddy dearest doesn't notice you're banging both his daughters?"

I turn to face him fully. "I don't share what's mine."

"Aurora isn't yours."

"Yet."

Penn raises his eyebrows. "Christ, you're worse than I thought. You do realize there's an entire city of beautiful women who don't come with this complication?"

"I don't want them."

"So, what happens when the Harrison family realizes you're playing them?"

I smile. "By then, it will be too late for anyone to do anything about it."

Penn sighs, the usual mischievous glint fading from his eyes. It's rare to see him this serious. He's our resident chaos agent, always finding humor in the darkest situations, but not now.

"Look, I know you think you're untouchable, but Derek Harrison isn't someone to fuck with." He lowers his voice. "The man built his empire by crushing anyone who crossed him. Even with your resources, he could make things... complicated."

"Complicated again?" I raise an eyebrow. "Thought we established that's just code for insufficient planning."

"I'm being serious, Hunt." Penn runs a hand through his already disheveled hair. "Harrison connections run deeper than even our network. The political capital alone—"

"I'm aware of Derek's reach." I check the monitor, noting Hansen's approach to the testing room. "Which is precisely why I'm handling this with care."

"Somehow, I doubt seducing his stepdaughter while engaged to his other daughter qualifies as care."

I turn from the screens to face him directly. "You're overthinking this. The engagement will be broken before Derek ever discovers my interest in Aurora."

"And how exactly do you plan to manage that without nuclear fallout?"

"I have options." I straighten my cuffs, a habit when strategizing. "Olivia breaks it off, decides I'm not the one. Or perhaps a scandal makes me unsuitable. Either way, the engagement ends, appropriate time passes, and then Aurora."

Penn shakes his head. "That simple, huh?"

"It's always simple when you control all variables."

"Except the human ones. Those tend to be messier."

I smile thinly. "Humans are predictable when you understand what drives them."

The intercom buzzes, alerting us that Hansen has arrived downstairs. Penn pushes off the control panel but pauses before heading to the door.

"And what drives Derek Harrison? Because whatever game you're playing, he's the one with the most power to destroy you."

I check my watch, checking how long until Hansen's fear test begins. "Derek's predictable. His weaknesses are obvious to anyone paying attention."

"The man built a billion-dollar empire. I wouldn't call that weak."

"I didn't say he was weak. I said his weaknesses are obvious." I pull up Hansen's file on the tablet. "Derek cares for his daughters, I'll admit that much. But he loves money and power more. He's addicted to it."

"Like you're not?" Penn challenges.

I ignore the comparison. "The difference is I recognize my addictions. Derek believes his actions are justified because they're wrapped in the veneer of family legacy. Everything he does, including this arranged marriage, is about expanding his empire, not securing his daughters' happiness."

"You think Aurora knows that?"

"She suspects. Olivia is blinded by daddy's approval." I scroll through Hansen's psychological profile. "That's why Derek chose her for this arrangement. She's malleable, eager to please. Aurora would have questioned his motives."

"So you're banking on Derek's greed outweighing his paternal instincts when this all goes to hell?"

I look up from the tablet. "It's not banking when it's a certainty. The man auctioned off his own daughter in a business merger disguised as an engagement. When faced with choosing between his empire and his daughters' feelings, Derek will always choose power."

Penn frowns. "Cold assessment."

"It's accurate. I respect Derek's business acumen, but let's not pretend this arrangement was born from anything but mutual gain. He wants my technology patents and market position. I wanted..." I pause, recalibrating. "I initially wanted his political connections."

"And now?"

I set down the tablet. "Now I want something he values far less than his empire."

"Hansen is here," Penn confirms, checking the security feed.

I nod, watching as the door to the testing chamber slides open. Hansen steps inside with measured movements, his gaze immediately taking in every detail of the room.

Unlike Sullivan, there's no visible anxiety in his posture. His file indicated severe claustrophobia, but you wouldn't know it from his composed demeanor. Interesting.

"This one might actually have potential," I murmur, studying his face on the monitor.

The testing chamber is one of my more elegant creations. It's a perfect twelve-by-twelve room with hydraulic walls that can reduce the space to a three-foot cube at the press of a button. For someone with claustrophobia, it's the ultimate nightmare.

I lean toward the microphone. "Mr. Hansen, welcome to

your evaluation." My voice echoes through the chamber. "As you've been informed, each candidate must face their greatest fear. Yours is rather straightforward."

Hansen doesn't flinch. No nervous tic, no rapid breathing. There is nothing to betray the anxiety he must be feeling.

"The walls will now begin to close in," I continue. "They will stop when you use the safeword 'terminate.' But using it means termination from the selection process as well. Understood?"

"Understood," Hansen replies, his voice steady.

I press the button to initiate the sequence. The hydraulic hiss fills the room as all four walls begin their slow advance.

Most candidates immediately track the walls, their eyes darting frantically as their breathing accelerates. Not Hansen. He stares dead ahead, almost in a trance, as if the walls aren't moving at all.

"Impressive," Penn mutters. "Think he's using some sort of meditation technique?"

I observe Hansen's unchanging expression as the room shrinks around him. "Perhaps. Or he's completely dissociating."

Either way, I'm becoming increasingly confident that Hansen won't break. Even as the space contracts to half its original size, a point where Sullivan would have been screaming, Hansen remains still, his face a mask of perfect control.

"This one's different," I say quietly. "One of the strongest candidates I've seen in a while."

The walls continue to close in, now compressing the space to barely six feet square. Most candidates would be hyperventilating by now. Hansen's breathing remains measured, controlled. His eyes stay fixed on a single point as the walls inch closer.

Four feet square. The room is now smaller than an elevator. Still nothing from Hansen.

Penn leans forward, fascination overtaking his usual bored expression. "How much further will you push him?"

"Until he breaks or succeeds." I watch the timer. Five minutes have passed. "Most candidates use the safeword within the first two minutes."

The hydraulics hiss as the walls reach the three-foot mark. Hansen is now standing in what amounts to a concrete coffin. His shoulders touch the walls on either side. He closes his eyes, a single bead of sweat rolling down his temple.

But still no safeword.

"Three more minutes," I announce into the microphone.

He doesn't acknowledge me. Doesn't need to. His mind is somewhere else entirely.

When the final seconds tick down, I stop the walls. Hansen opens his eyes, the only indication he's even aware that the test has ended.

"Congratulations, Mr. Hansen. You've passed." I release the mechanism, and the walls slide back to their original position.

Hansen takes a single deep breath, his first visible reaction to the ordeal. He straightens his tie, nods once at the camera, and walks toward the exit with steady steps.

"Seven candidates remaining," Penn notes, marking his tablet. "That's enough for the final phase."

"I trust you can make the arrangements for them to convene at my estate tomorrow night," I say, shutting down the monitoring system. "Ten o'clock. Ensure they understand this is the point of no return."

Penn nods. "I'll handle it. Any special instructions for their preparation?"

"Tell them to pack as if they're never coming back." I collect my jacket. "Some of them won't be."

I head for the exit, my mind already mapping out tomorrow's trials. My estate's isolation makes it perfect for the breaking point—the final test that will determine which candidates truly belong among the Vipers.

Time to prepare.

13

AURORA

I stand at the edge of the property, watching waves crash against the rocks below. I came here to clear my head, but the turmoil followed me to my father's cliff house.

I wrap my arms around myself, shivering despite the afternoon sun. This place used to bring me peace. Now it only reminds me of Hunter pulling me back from the edge that day. His hands were on my waist. His breath was on my neck.

God, I'm pathetic.

My phone buzzes in my pocket—the sixth text from Olivia since this morning. I can't bring myself to look. The lie about a work assignment in Portland sits like poison in my stomach. I've never lied to her before, not about anything important.

"Just a quick weekend trip for an author interview," I'd told her yesterday, watching her face fall with disappointment.

"But we were supposed to look at floral arrangements tomorrow," she'd said, her voice small.

The memory makes me wince. I couldn't stand another minute of wedding talk, especially not when every mention of Hunter's name makes me feel like I'm drowning.

I turn away from the cliff edge and head back inside. The house is too quiet, too empty. Just me and my thoughts and the ghost of my father in every room.

In the kitchen, I pour a glass of wine even though it's barely past noon. The red liquid swirls as my hand trembles. I've spent my entire life being the reliable one, the strong one. Now I'm hiding from my own sister because I can't face what I've done.

The truth is, I don't know what scares me more—the possibility that Hunter might reveal our secret, or the terrifying realization that part of me doesn't want him to stop pursuing me.

I take a long sip, letting the wine burn down my throat. What am I supposed to do now? Tell Olivia everything and destroy her? Keep this horrible secret and let it destroy me instead?

I sink into a chair at the kitchen table, resting my forehead against the cool wood. I came here looking for answers, but all I've found is the same impossible choice waiting for me.

I carry my wine to the living room, drawn to the large picture window that frames the ocean like a living painting. The view has always calmed me, even after my father jumped—the endless blue stretching to meet the sky, waves foaming white against the rocks below. Today, it only reminds me how trapped I feel.

I press my forehead against the cool glass, wine glass clasped loosely in my fingers. The afternoon sun glints off the water, almost blinding.

That's when I see him.

A dark figure appears at the cliff edge, hands in pockets, staring out at the horizon. My breath catches in my throat. Hunter. Even at this distance, I'd know that posture anywhere—tall, commanding, like he owns not just the land beneath his feet but the very air around him.

My muscles tense instantly, heart hammering against my ribs. What is he doing here? How did he know I'd be at the cliff house?

As if sensing my thoughts, Hunter turns, his gaze lifting toward the house. Our eyes meet through the glass, and the wine glass nearly slips from my fingers. There's no mistaking it. He sees me watching him. Even from this distance, I can feel the weight of his stare, that same intensity that's been haunting my dreams.

I step back from the window, but it's too late. A small, knowing smile curves his lips, and he gives a slight nod of acknowledgment. My skin prickles with goosebumps despite the warmth of the room.

He's here at the same time as me, whether that's a coincidence or not remains to be seen.

And now he's caught me watching him.

Less than two minutes go by, and the doorbell rings, making my heart rate spike uncontrollably.

The sound of the doorbell still hangs in the air when Martha's footsteps echo across the foyer. I stand frozen, wine glass clutched in my hand like a shield. Maybe it isn't him. Maybe I'm jumping to conclusions.

"I need to see Aurora." Hunter's voice, low and commanding. "Now."

My stomach drops to the floor. Martha's gentle voice responds, too quiet for me to make out the words, but I can imagine her polite hesitation.

"She's here." Hunter's tone brooks no argument. "Her car is outside."

I set the wine glass down with trembling fingers, spilling a few drops on the table. There's nowhere to run. We're miles from anywhere, perched on this lonely cliff with nothing but ocean below and winding roads above.

"Miss Aurora?" Martha calls out, her voice wavering. "Mr. Reed is here to see you."

I smooth my hands over my sweater, heart hammering so loudly I'm certain he'll hear it when he enters. What does he want? Why follow me here? The questions swarm like angry bees in my mind.

"It's fine, Martha," I call back, my voice betraying me with a slight crack. "You can head home. I'll lock up later."

"Are you sure, Miss?" Concern laces her words.

Before I can respond, Hunter's voice cuts in. "She's sure."

Footsteps approach the living room. I force myself to remain standing, to face him, even as every instinct screams at me to hide.

Martha appears in the doorway, wringing her hands. "Miss Aurora, I can stay if you'd like."

Behind her, Hunter's tall frame fills the hallway, gray-blue eyes locked on mine with an intensity that makes my skin flush hot despite the chill in my veins.

"That won't be necessary," Hunter says, never breaking his gaze from mine.

Martha hesitates, looking between us uncertainly before nodding. "I'll see you tomorrow then."

The front door closes moments later, the sound echoing with finality through the house. We're alone. Completely alone.

Hunter steps into the living room, and suddenly the space feels too small, the air too thin.

"Aurora," he says my name like he owns it.

I cross my arms over my chest. "What are you doing here?"

Hunter strolls farther into the room, his gaze sweeping over the ocean view before returning to me. "Interesting coincidence, finding you here today."

"This is my father's house. I have every right to be here."

"I didn't say you didn't." His lips quirk into that half-smile that makes my pulse race against my will. "But the timing is... inconvenient."

"For who? You?" I lift my chin. "I'm not going anywhere."

Hunter slides his hands into his pockets, studying me. "I'm hosting a gathering this evening. At my property. A private initiation for a select group of people."

"And this concerns me how?"

"Our properties share this section of the coastline." He gestures toward the window. "Sound carries. You might hear things... and see things you shouldn't."

Understanding dawns. "So that's why you're here? To warn me away from my own family's property?"

"I'm simply suggesting discretion." His eyes darken. "In fact, I'd need you to sign an NDA if you're planning to stay."

"An NDA?" I laugh, the sound sharp and brittle. "You must be joking."

"I never joke about business, Aurora."

"This isn't business. This is me sleeping in my father's home." I step closer, anger replacing my earlier nervousness. "I'm not signing anything. If you're concerned about your little 'initiation,' maybe you should hold it somewhere more private."

Hunter's jaw tightens. "You don't understand what you're refusing."

"I understand perfectly. You think your secret boys' club trumps my right to be here." I gesture toward the door. "I have no interest in whatever you and your friends are doing. But I'm not leaving, and I'm certainly not signing anything."

Hunter's expression darkens. In three swift strides, he closes the distance between us, backing me against the wall. His palm slams against the surface beside my head, the sound making me flinch.

"Let me be clear." His voice drops to a dangerous whisper. "This isn't a request."

My breath catches in my throat. He's hovering inches from my face, close enough that I can feel the heat radiating from his body. His eyes have turned stormy, and all traces of civility have vanished.

"You don't intimidate me," I say, but my voice betrays me, coming out breathless and shaky.

Hunter's lips curve into a cruel smile. "Your pulse says otherwise." His free hand comes up to trace my neck, fingers pressing against the frantic beating beneath my skin. "I can feel how fast your heart is racing."

I should be terrified. I should be pushing him away, screaming, doing anything but standing here letting him touch me. Instead, heat pools low in my belly, an unwelcome, traitorous response.

"I always get what I want, Aurora." His thumb brushes across my bottom lip, rough and possessive. "One way or another."

"Is this how you treat all women who tell you no?" I manage to ask, hating how breathy I sound.

"Only the ones who need to understand their place."

God help me, something about his dominance sends a thrill through me. What kind of person am I becoming? What kind of woman gets turned on by threats from her sister's fiancé?

"This is wrong," I whisper

"Maybe." He leans closer, his breath hot against my ear. "But your pupils are dilated, Aurora. Your breathing is shallow. You like this."

I close my eyes, ashamed because he's right. Every cell in my body is responding to him, screaming for his touch even as my mind recoils at his methods.

"Tell me I'm wrong," he challenges, his hand sliding to grip my waist.

I say nothing, can't say anything. The truth is written all over my body.

"Sign the NDA, Aurora." Hunter's voice drops lower, a seductive rumble against my ear. "Stay for tonight."

I try to turn my face away, but his fingers catch my chin, forcing me to look at him. "Why would I want to?"

"Because what happens here tonight..." His thumb brushes across my bottom lip, sending unwanted shivers down my spine. "It's the kind of thing you pretend to abhor in the daylight but crave in your darkest moments."

My heart hammers against my ribs. "You don't know anything about me."

"Don't I?" His smile is predatory. "I see the darkness in you, Aurora. The same darkness I recognized that day on the cliff. You weren't just trying to understand your father's suicide, you were feeling the pull yourself."

I suck in a breath. No one has ever seen through me like this.

"Tonight is about testing limits." His hand slides down my throat to rest at the hollow of my collarbone. "What we do is sick and depraved by society's standards. Men hunting men. The final test of worthiness."

"Hunting?" The word barely escapes my lips.

"The candidates who survive become part of something greater than themselves." His fingers trace patterns on my skin. "People who've wronged us, betrayed us. They serve a purpose in the end."

Horror mingles with a forbidden curiosity I can't suppress. "You're talking about killing people."

"I'm talking about justice." His lips brush my ear. "But I'm offering you something different. A hunt where you're the prey."

My breath catches. "What?"

"Sign the NDA. Stay on your property tonight. I'll give you a head start—one hour to hide anywhere on these grounds." His eyes gleam with dark promise. "And then I'll come find you."

"And when you find me?" I shouldn't be asking. I shouldn't want to know.

"Then I claim my prize." His hand slides to my waist, gripping possessively. "And I promise, Aurora, you'll enjoy every second of surrendering to me."

I hate that his words make heat pool between my thighs. Hate that he sees the part of me I've tried so desperately to bury. A piece of me that craves the edge of danger, that wants to be taken and claimed.

"You're sick," I whisper.

"Maybe." His smile widens. "But so are you. That's why we're perfect for each other."

Hunter reaches into his jacket pocket and pulls out an official-looking document, holding it up between us. "So what's it going to be, Aurora? Will you sign the NDA or not?"

I stare at the paper, my mouth suddenly dry. "You just happen to have that with you?"

"I'm always prepared." His lips curve into that arrogant smile that makes my stomach flip.

"Why would you carry an NDA around? Do you make a habit of forcing women to sign legal documents?"

Hunter's eyes darken. "Trust me when I say you don't want to know."

I swallow hard, reaching for the document with trembling fingers. My eyes scan over the legal jargon—confidentiality clauses, non-disclosure requirements, severe penalties for breaches. This is madness. I should throw it back in his face and walk out.

But I don't.

"Do you have a pen?" I hear myself asking.

Hunter studies me for a long moment, as if seeing something in me I've tried to hide from everyone else. "You surprise me. Most people would be running by now."

"Maybe I'm not most people."

"No," he says softly, pulling a sleek black pen from his inner pocket. "You're not."

The weight of the pen feels significant in my hand, like I'm about to sign away more than just my silence. I hesitate, pen hovering above the signature line.

"Having second thoughts?" Hunter challenges.

"A million of them." I meet his gaze. "But you are right about me. The darkness you saw in me that day on the cliff... It's real."

Hunter's expression shifts, something unreadable flickering in his eyes. "We recognize our own kind."

Something about his words resonates in a place I've kept locked away. The truth is, I've always felt different, always sensed a shadow inside me that normal people don't possess. The proper thing would be to walk away, to run from whatever twisted game he's proposing.

Instead, I press the pen to paper and sign my name.

14

HUNTER

I turn the skull mask over in my hands, tracing my fingers along its contours. The smooth, bone-white surface gleams under the light of my study. Perfect for tonight's hunt. Not the Selection hunt that the others are expecting me to lead, but something far more personal.

"You're really not joining us tonight?" Penn leans against my desk, arms crossed. "The candidates are expecting all five of us."

"They'll have to make do with four." I place the mask in my bag alongside the other items I've prepared. Rope. A knife. A small first aid kit. Everything a proper hunter might need.

Grayson's eyes narrow as he watches me pack. "The final phase is crucial. We need you there."

"You're more than capable of handling it without me." I zip the bag closed with finality. "I have other plans."

"Other plans?" Ari raises an eyebrow, his usual smooth demeanor tinged with surprise. "Tonight of all nights?"

I check my watch. Aurora's head start has begun. My blood already pulses with anticipation, imagining her running through the darkened estate, heart racing, adrenaline flooding her system.

"I have a date with the woman next door." I can't help the smile that curls my lips.

"Next door?" Penn straightens. "You mean Aurora Harrison?"

I don't answer, but my expression must confirm it.

"Fuck, Hunter." Grayson shakes his head. "You're engaged to her sister. Derek Harrison is one of the most powerful men in New York City."

"And?" I shoulder my bag.

Ari steps forward. "This path you're taking is reckless. Even for you."

"I know exactly what I'm doing." I slip my phone into my pocket. "Handle the logistics tonight. Make sure the final five are ready for induction tomorrow."

"Hunter—" Penn starts.

"It's done." My tone leaves no room for argument. "I've waited long enough for her."

I leave my colleagues behind, their concerns fading with distance as I make my way through the trees toward the Harrison estate. The night air feels electric against my skin. Aurora had an hour's head start, which is enough time to hide, to strategize, to let fear take hold.

Perfect.

The moon hangs low and full, casting long shadows across the manicured grounds. I move silently along the perimeter, every sense heightened. Hunting has always come naturally to me—in business, in pleasure. Tonight, the lines blur deliciously.

The Harrison mansion looms dark against the night sky. Not a single light shines from within its windows. Smart girl. Darkness is both shield and weapon, but she doesn't realize I've spent my life mastering the shadows.

I circle the eastern wing, where the cliff drops away to the churning ocean below. My eyes adjust to the darkness, scanning for movement, for the slightest disturbance in the natural order of things. For her.

Is she inside, hidden in some forgotten room? Or outside, crouched among the gardens, her breath held tight in her chest? The game thrills me because I don't know.

I pause at the edge of the back gardens, listening. The waves crash below, wind rustles through leaves, but beneath it all, there's nothing. No footsteps, no breathing, no telltale signs of panic.

Continuing my circuit around the property, I pass by the pool house, its glass walls reflecting moonlight. Empty. The boathouse at the edge of the property reveals nothing but shadows and silence.

I check my watch. The head start has ended, and I know she's going to make me work for it. I smile in the darkness, appreciating her effort.

As I approach the west side of the house, a curtain in one of the downstairs windows moves just slightly.

Found you.

I'd hoped she would have chosen to hide outside. The thrill of the hunt is amplified in the open air—the sounds of footsteps on fallen leaves, the hitched breathing echoing in the night. But Aurora's smarter than that. She's barricaded herself in familiar territory.

No matter. I can drive her out.

Moving silently along the stone path, I approach the service entrance I noted during my earlier reconnaissance. It's an old door with an outdated lock that any halfway decent thief could bypass in seconds. I remove the lock pick set from my pocket, selecting the tension wrench and hook pick.

The metallic clicks sound unnaturally loud in the stillness as I work the pins. One by one, they yield to my touch, a satisfying metaphor for how Aurora herself will soon surrender. The final pin drops into place with a soft click, and I turn the handle.

The door swings open on well-oiled hinges. I step inside, my boots silent on the marble floor of what appears to be a mudroom. The house smells of furniture polish and expensive candles, with an underlying hint of sea salt from the nearby cliffs.

I pause, listening. The mansion is silent, but houses this size never truly sleep. They creak and settle, pipes hum, old wood expands and contracts. Among those natural sounds, I detect the faint rustle of movement from deeper within.

A smile spreads across my face as I move forward, keeping to the shadows. I've spent years perfecting the art of moving undetected, and tonight that skill serves a singular purpose.

A floorboard creaks somewhere above. Second floor, west wing, if I've oriented correctly. My pulse quickens. The hunt is on.

I make my way toward the grand staircase, pausing at its base to consider my approach. Direct pursuit might drive her further inside, into some hidden room or passage I'm unfamiliar with. Better to cut off her escape routes, force her toward the gardens where the real game can begin.

I pause at the base of the grand staircase, drinking in the silence. The game grows more enticing with each passing moment. I can almost taste her fear in the air—sweet, intoxicating.

"Aurora," I call, my voice echoing through the empty halls. "You're only making this more exciting for me."

I listen carefully, rewarded by the faintest intake of breath from somewhere upstairs. The sound sends a thrill through my body, straight to my cock. She's trying so hard to stay silent, but it's difficult when adrenaline is pumping through your veins.

Ascending the stairs, I let each footfall announce my approach. I want her to hear me coming. I want her to feel the inevitable closing in.

"I can hear you breathing," I say, softer now. "Your heart must be racing. Does it excite you to be hunted? Knowing what will happen when I find you?"

Another sound—fabric shifting against skin. She's moving. The hunt quickens.

I follow the sound down the hallway, each step measured. The carpet absorbs my footfalls, allowing me to move more silently now. I pass darkened doorways, checking each room.

"When I catch you," I murmur into the darkness, "and I will catch you, I'm going to take what's mine."

She gasps, quickly trying to stifle it. Close—she's very close. The sound came from behind the door to my right. I press my palm against the wood, feeling the cool surface against my skin.

"I wonder what you're wearing," I continue. "Did you dress for me? Or will I have the pleasure of tearing whatever it is from your body?"

I turn the handle of the door that I'm sure she's lurking behind, slowly, deliberately, giving her time to anticipate. The door creaks open to reveal a darkened bedroom. Moonlight spills through open curtains, casting long shadows across the floor.

The closet door stands slightly ajar. A rookie mistake.

I approach, blood rushing in my veins. The thrill of the chase narrows my focus to this single moment, this impending capture.

"I can smell your perfume," I whisper, close enough to the closet that she'll hear every word. "And something else. Are you wet for me already, baby? Aroused by this game we're playing?"

I reach for the closet handle, a smirk spreading across my face. The hunt is about to end, or so I think.

The sudden movement behind me registers a fraction too late. Aurora slams the bedroom door, the wood catching my shoulder as I spin around. Clever girl. She wasn't in the closet at all. She was behind the door the entire time.

"Fuck!" I growl, shoving against the door and bursting into the hallway.

A flash of movement catches my eye, Aurora's slender figure darting down the corridor, her dark hair flying behind her. The sight of her fleeing ignites something dark in me. The real chase begins.

I launch after her, my longer stride eating up the distance between us. Her breathing comes in quick, panicked gasps that echo off the walls. The sound drives me wild.

"You can't outrun me, Aurora," I call, my voice bouncing through the hallway. "Every step just makes me want you more."

She glances back, her blue eyes wide with a mixture of fear and excitement. That single look confirms what I already knew. She wants this as much as I do.

Aurora reaches the staircase, taking the steps two at a time. Her body moves with unexpected grace under pressure. I'm close enough now to catch the scent of her perfume mixed with sweat and arousal. My cock hardens painfully against my jeans.

"The longer you run, the harder I'll fuck you when I catch you," I promise, my voice dropping to a dangerous register.

She stumbles slightly on the bottom step, and I lunge forward. My fingers graze the back of her shirt, so close, but she twists away at the last second, veering toward the kitchen.

"That's it, baby. Make me work for it," I growl, the near-miss only heightening my arousal.

The chase narrows my world to just her—the sound of her rapid breathing, the flash of skin as her top rides up, the way her ass moves as she runs. Every cell in my body screams to possess her.

I'm gaining on her with each step, close enough to feel the heat radiating from her body. The chase has my blood singing; every instinct is focused on capturing my prey. Aurora darts into the kitchen, her hands fumbling for the light switch. Smart. She's looking for weapons, for barriers to put between us.

I laugh softly. "Nothing in there will save you."

She whirls around, back pressed against the marble countertop. The moonlight streaming through the windows casts her face in silver and shadow. Her chest heaves with each breath, lips parted, eyes wide. Fucking perfect.

"You're cornered," I say, moving deliberately toward her. "Game over."

"Stay back," she warns, her hand closing around a kitchen knife from the block behind her.

The sight of steel in her trembling hand only heightens

my arousal. I step closer, watching her grip tighten on the handle.

"Would you use that on me, Aurora?" I ask, advancing another step. "I don't think you would."

Her eyes dart to the doorway behind me, assessing her chances. I shift slightly to block her path, enjoying how her gaze tracks my movement.

"You signed the agreement," I remind her, now close enough to smell her perfume mixed with fear-sweat. "You knew what would happen when I caught you."

"I didn't think—" she starts, voice breaking.

"Yes, you did." I take another step forward. "You knew exactly what you were agreeing to. What you wanted."

The knife wavers in her hand. I reach out slowly, wrapping my fingers around her wrist. Her pulse jumps wildly beneath my touch.

"Drop it," I command softly.

For a moment, resistance flashes in her eyes. It's that defiance that drew me to her from the start. Then, with a soft clatter, the knife falls to the floor.

I kick it away without breaking eye contact. "Good girl."

15

AURORA

My back presses against the cold marble countertop as Hunter looms over me, his body effectively caging mine. The knife I held seconds ago now lies uselessly on the floor, kicked away by his quick movements. I can't believe I grabbed it, and I can't believe I dropped it so easily at his command.

"Nowhere to run now," Hunter murmurs, his voice a deep rumble that vibrates through my chest.

My breath comes in shallow gasps as Hunter towers over me. It's only now that I notice he's wearing a mask—a skull design that covers the upper half of his face. The white bone pattern contrasts sharply with his dark attire, making his gray-blue eyes burn even more intensely through the eye holes.

Despite the absurdity of the situation, his hunting me through my dad's house, there's something undeniably alluring about the mask. The way it transforms him from a billionaire businessman into a dangerous predator.

"Why the mask?" I manage to ask, my voice steadier than I expected.

Hunter tilts his head slightly, studying me. His mouth —the only part of his face visible below the skull design— curves into a slow smile.

"Anonymity," he says, reaching up to touch the edge of it. "Though I suppose that's pointless with you."

My eyes trace the contours of the skull, the way it accentuates the sharp angles of his jawline. I wonder if he plans to keep it on for whatever comes next. The thought sends an unexpected shiver through me.

"Do you like it?" Hunter asks, noticing my lingering gaze. He moves closer, eliminating what little space remains between us. "Does it scare you, Aurora?"

"No," I lie, my back pressing harder against the counter as I try to maintain some distance. "I'm not scared of you."

His laugh is low and knowing. "Your pulse says otherwise." His fingers brush against my neck, finding my racing heartbeat. "But it's not just fear, is it?"

I swallow hard, unable to deny the contradictory emotions swirling within. Terror and excitement tangle together in ways I can't separate.

"Why the hunt? Why the mask?" I press again, desperate to understand what's happening between us. "Is this all just a game to you?"

Hunter places both hands on the counter, truly boxing me in. His breath fans across my face, warm through the mask's mouth opening.

"A game?" His voice drops. "Games have rules, Aurora. Rules can be bent." He leans closer, his masked face inches from mine. "This is more... primal."

My heart hammers against my ribs. The kitchen suddenly feels too small, the air too thick.

"Then what is it?" I challenge, though my voice betrays me with a slight tremble.

"A hunt requires instinct." One of his hands moves to my waist, fingers pressing into my hip with possessive pressure. "Like what's between us. Pure instinct."

I should push him away. I should run. I should remember Olivia. But my body refuses to obey what my mind knows is right.

"I don't have those instincts," I lie.

Hunter's laugh is dark, knowing. "Your eyes say otherwise." His thumb traces my bottom lip, and I hate how my mouth parts slightly at his touch. "Your body says otherwise."

"This doesn't make sense," I whisper, more to myself than him.

"Doesn't it?" His other hand slides up my neck, cupping my jaw. "From the moment I pulled you from that cliff, I knew."

"Knew what?"

His eyes bore into mine through the mask. "That you're mine."

The possessiveness in his voice should repulse me. Instead, it ignites something deep and dangerous.

"I'm not yours," I say, but it sounds hollow even to my own ears. "I can't be."

"Can't? Or won't?" His thumb strokes my cheek, surprisingly gentle for a predator. "There's a difference."

My hands remain flat against the counter behind me, neither pushing him away nor pulling him closer. I'm frozen in my own contradiction.

"You promised me a prize," Hunter says, his voice dropping to a whisper. "I've caught you."

In this moment of twisted intimacy, I see my opportunity. Hunter's entirely focused on my face, his hands preoccupied with caging me in. His stance is wide, confident.

"You're right," I whisper, letting my body soften. His eyes flash with triumph behind the skull mask.

That's when I strike.

I drive my knee upward with all my strength, connecting solidly with his groin. Hunter doubles over with a guttural sound that's half-roar, half-gasp. The mighty predator, suddenly reduced to something mortal.

"You just fucking—" he chokes out, but I'm already moving.

I shove past him while he's still hunched over, adrenaline surging through my veins. My feet slip slightly on the polished kitchen floor as I sprint toward the hallway. Behind me, I hear Hunter's labored breathing, followed by a string of curses that would make a sailor blush.

The front door is just ahead. My escape. My lungs burn as I push myself faster, hands already reaching for the handle. Just a few more steps and I'll be outside, away from this madness, away from him.

"Run out that door," Hunter's voice booms from behind me, the pain in it replaced by something darker, "and I'll have a fucking field day with you outside."

I hesitate, my fingers mere inches from the handle. The threat in his voice is unmistakable, but there's something else too—a promise. Out there in the darkness, away from the confines of walls and ceilings, he'd truly be the predator he's pretending to be. And I would be truly cornered.

I freeze with my hand on the doorknob, Hunter's threat echoing in my ears. My pulse thunders at my temples as a realization washes over me. I don't want this to end.

The reasonable part of my brain screams at me to stop, to remember Olivia, to remember all the reasons this is wrong. But beneath that voice is something darker, something I've been denying since the moment Hunter pulled me from that cliff edge.

I want him to chase me.

"What's it going to be, Aurora?" Hunter's voice is closer now, recovered enough to move toward me. The skull mask makes him look inhuman in the dim hallway light.

I meet his eyes through the mask's openings and see the challenge there. The hunt isn't over. It's barely begun.

My lips curve into a smile as I throw the door open and launch myself into the night.

The cool air hits my flushed skin as I race down the front steps. Behind me, I hear Hunter's curse of surprise, followed by the thunder of his footsteps. He didn't expect this. He thought his threat would make me surrender.

But I'm done surrendering.

The grounds stretch before me. Shadowy gardens, winding paths, and hidden corners. Perfect for a hunt. Perfect for us.

"You're making this so much worse for yourself," Hunter calls from behind me, his voice carrying across the darkness. There's a note of appreciation there, of respect for my boldness.

I don't respond, saving my breath as I cut across the lawn toward the gardens. My heart pounds not with fear but with exhilaration. This is complete madness, but I've never felt more alive.

The thrill of being pursued, of being wanted this desperately, burns through my veins like fire. Hunter doesn't want my sister. He doesn't want anyone but me. And God help me, I want him to catch me.

Just not too easily.

I dart across the moonlit lawn, my feet finding familiar paths even in the darkness. I spent summers here as a child, memorizing every garden path, every hidden alcove. My father's estate has been my playground long before it became the setting for this dangerous game.

Hunter's footsteps thunder behind me, but I have the advantage of knowledge. I cut sharply left, ducking behind the old stone gazebo, then race along the hedge maze's exterior rather than entering its confusing pathways. A rookie mistake would be getting trapped inside those green walls.

"You can't outrun me forever," Hunter calls, his voice closer than I'd like.

I push harder, my lungs burning as I sprint toward the rose garden. There's an archway there with dense climbing vines. As I dash through it, I deliberately veer away from the eastern path that would lead to the cliffs.

No. Not there. Never there.

The cliff edge where my father jumped, where Hunter first found me—it holds too much meaning, too much pain. Running there would feel like fate closing a circle I'm not ready to complete. Besides, the cliff offers nowhere to hide, nowhere to run. Just the final edge of everything.

Instead, I follow the winding path through the willow grove, where drooping branches create curtains of green. The soft ground muffles my footsteps as I weave between the ancient trunks. My childhood hiding spots flash through my mind like signposts. The hollow log by the stream, the stone bench obscured by ferns, the gardener's shed with its broken lock.

I slow my pace just enough to quiet my breathing, listening for Hunter's pursuit. For a moment, there's nothing but night sounds—crickets chirping, leaves rustling. Then a twig snaps to my right, and I freeze.

He's closer than I thought. And he's not following the path.

I change direction, heading for the terraced gardens with their multiple levels and stone staircases. My heart pounds against my ribs, partly from exertion but mostly from the thrill of this chase. There's something exhilarating about being pursued through these gardens that have witnessed generations of secrets.

The moonlight spills across the manicured lawns, illuminating my way but also exposing my position. I need cover, shadows. Somewhere to disappear.

I dart between rows of heritage rosebushes, their thorns catching at my clothes like grasping fingers. My lungs burn with each breath, but I can't slow down. Hunter's footsteps have quieted. The predator is switching tactics, and that terrifies me more than his thundering pursuit.

Beyond the terraced gardens lies my best chance at escape: the small woodland that marks the far boundary of the estate. It's not quite a forest, more a dense collection of trees my father preserved when developing the property. As a child, I called it the Wildwood, building forts between ancient oaks and playing hide-and-seek among ferns with my parents before the fateful day. After that day, I rarely visited until I got older.

If I can reach it, the dense undergrowth and tight spaces between trees might give me an advantage. Hunter's broader frame would struggle where I could slip through. The darkness would become my ally rather than my enemy.

I glance over my shoulder, seeing nothing but moonlit gardens. He's still out there, though. I feel his presence like a physical weight against my skin.

The woodland seems impossibly far now, a dark smudge against the night sky. My legs tremble with exertion, a stitch forming in my side that tightens with each breath. Track team captain for three years in high school, cross-country runner in college—none of it prepared me for this.

This isn't about form, endurance, or beating personal records. This is pure survival instinct; my body pushed beyond its limits by desperation. In track, I knew the finish line, understood the rules, and recognized my competitors. Here, the only rule is don't get caught, and my competitor is a man who makes predators look tame.

I push myself harder, ignoring the burning in my thighs and the ragged sound of my breathing. The gap between the manicured gardens and the wild tangle of trees grows smaller. Twenty more seconds and I'll reach the first line of pines that mark the woodland's edge.

A twig snaps somewhere to my left.

I don't look. Looking slows you down. But my heartbeat skitters wildly as I realize Hunter isn't behind me at all.

He's cutting me off.

16

HUNTER

I circle through the dense undergrowth, moving fast and silent. Years of hunting have taught me patience and how to track prey. And Aurora Harrison is the most exquisite prey I've ever pursued.

The moonlight catches on her hair as she darts between the rose bushes, unaware I've cut around to intercept her path. My blood pumps harder watching her run—the determination in every step, the clever way she uses the terrain. She's not panicking. She's thinking. Planning. Fighting.

Fuck, that turns me on.

Lesser women would have surrendered at the first sign of pursuit, hoping clemency might follow submission. Not Aurora. She fights, challenges, and refuses to yield even when cornered.

I slip between twin oaks, positioning myself ahead of her intended path toward the woodland. Her breathing is coming in quick, shallow pants that make my cock strain against my pants. The sound of prey pushing its limits, testing its capabilities against a superior predator.

The woodland she's aiming for would give her an advantage—tighter spaces, more places to hide. Smart girl. But I know these grounds almost as well as she does. I've studied every inch of this property as well as my own.

I crouch lower as she approaches, her silhouette visible through the sparse trees marking the boundary between manicured gardens and wild growth. She's slowing slightly, her hand pressed against the stitch in her side. Even in pain, she moves with grace, determination etched into every line of her body.

My fingers itch to trace those lines, to map the geography of her surrender.

This isn't just desire. This is raw hunger. I want to consume her, possess her completely. And her resistance, her refusal to surrender easily, only intensifies that need.

I shift positions, ready to intercept. She's close now, eyes fixed on the woodland ahead, unaware that her sanctuary has become her trap. The wild tangle of trees she thinks will hide her will, in fact, witness her capture.

She doesn't see me yet, but she will. And when she does, when our eyes meet, and she realizes I've outmaneuvered her, that moment will be sweeter than any conquest I've known before.

A twig snaps beneath my boot, a tactical error that sends Aurora's head whipping in my direction. Her eyes widen with fear when she realizes I'm not behind her. I'm right here, waiting.

One second. That's all it takes.

I lunge forward, capturing her slim wrist in my hand. Her momentum carries forward even as I yank her backward, spinning her around before slamming her against the ancient oak. My body pins hers completely, her chest crushed against rough bark, my much larger frame eliminating any possibility of escape.

She screams. A sound that pierces the quiet night and shoots straight to my groin. The vibration of it travels through her body into mine, and I press harder against her, one hand capturing both wrists above her head.

"I told you running would make things worse," I growl against her ear, feeling her shudder. "But I'm so fucking glad you did."

Her fear is intoxicating—the rapid rise and fall of her breath, the trembling of her limbs, the way she squirms against me only to discover there's nowhere to go. My cock hardens instantly, pressing against the curve of her ass through my pants. I roll my hips, making sure she feels exactly what she does to me.

"Feel that?" I ask, my voice dropping lower. "That's what your little game of chase did."

Another desperate sound escapes her throat—halfway between a whimper and another scream. I press my lips against the exposed skin of her neck, drinking in the salt of her perspiration.

"Go ahead and scream again," I encourage, scraping my teeth along her skin. "No one can hear you out here. It's just us."

My free hand slides around her waist, pulling her hips back more firmly against me.

"I caught you, Aurora," I murmur against her ear. "Now you're mine."

Aurora's hips push back against me, the curve of her ass grinding against my hardened cock, and a groan rips from my throat. Even pinned against this tree, completely at my mercy, she can't hide her desire.

"You're a fucking naughty girl," I growl into her ear,

tightening my grip on her wrists. "Wanting your sister's fiancé so badly."

Her entire body tenses at my words, muscles going rigid beneath my touch. That's exactly what I want, to witness that delicious conflict. The taboo of what we're doing only heightens the thrill.

"That's right," I continue, my breath hot against her neck. "Think about it. Think about Olivia planning our wedding while her sister gets fucked by her future husband."

She whimpers, the sound caught between protest and arousal. My free hand slides around to the front of her jeans, finding the button. She didn't make this easy on me by wearing tight denim instead of something I could easily tear away.

I pop the button open with ease, then drag the zipper down slowly, savoring each metallic click. Her breathing quickens as I hook my fingers into both her jeans and panties, tugging them down with a rough jerk. The cool night air hits her exposed skin, raising goosebumps I can feel beneath my fingers.

"Look at you," I murmur, sliding my hand between her legs from behind. "Fighting so hard, running so fast, but your cunt knows exactly what it wants."

My fingers find her pussy, soaked and hot despite her protests. I slide two fingers through her slick folds, collecting her wetness, before pushing them inside her tight heat.

"Fucking sopping wet," I growl, curling my fingers forward to find that spot that makes her cry out. "Your cunt doesn't lie, baby. It knows you're mine."

The wetness coating my fingers ignites something animalistic inside me. The hunt, the chase, her resistance has awakened something feral in my blood. I spin her around, her back now pressed against the rough bark, and drop to my knees before her.

"What are you—" she starts, but her words dissolve into a gasp as I yank her jeans and panties down further, exposing her completely to the moonlight.

Her pussy glistens in the silvery light, swollen and dripping with arousal that contradicts every protest that's left her mouth. The sight of her breaks something inside me. Any remaining restraint shatters.

"I need to taste you," I growl, my voice barely recognizable even to my own ears.

I grab her thighs, spreading them wider, forcing her to brace herself against the tree trunk. Without warning, I bury my face between her legs, my tongue flattening against her slit in one long, possessive lick.

"Fuck," I groan against her flesh, the taste of her flooding my senses. "So fucking sweet."

Her hands fly to my hair, torn between pushing me away and pulling me closer. I grip her thighs harder, ensuring she can't escape as I feast on her like a man starving. My tongue circles her clit before sucking it between my lips, drawing a broken cry from somewhere above me.

I devour her relentlessly, lapping at her wetness, drinking her in as though she's water and I've been wandering the desert. My tongue plunges inside her, then returns to her clit, alternating between penetrating her and circling that sensitive bundle of nerves.

Her thighs begin to tremble against my palms. I can feel her fighting the pleasure, fighting her own desire. Her hips buck against my mouth, seeking more contact, more pressure.

I look up from between her legs, watching her face

contort with unwanted pleasure as I consume her. Her eyes are squeezed shut, head thrown back against the tree, lip caught between her teeth as she tries to silence her moans.

I feel her pussy tightening against my tongue, her thighs trembling harder against my palms. She's so fucking close. Her fingers tangle in my hair, nails scraping my scalp as she fights the pleasure I'm forcing on her.

"Give it to me," I growl against her slick flesh.

When she still resists, I decide to push her over the edge. I suck her swollen clit between my lips and graze it with my teeth—just the slightest nip, the perfect balance of pain and pleasure.

The effect is instantaneous. Her entire body convulses, a strangled cry tearing from her throat as she comes violently against my mouth. Her pussy pulses and gushes, coating my tongue with her release as her body bucks uncontrollably.

Something in me snaps. All pretense of control evaporates, replaced by a hunger to claim this woman completely. I'm fucking driven by instinct.

I yank her jeans and panties down her legs, past her ankles, and over her shoes, tossing them carelessly aside. Standing quickly, I unbuckle my belt and free my cock with desperate, fumbling fingers. It springs out, rock hard and straining, the head already leaking.

Before she can recover from her orgasm, I grip her waist and lift her against the tree. Her back scrapes against rough bark as I position her pussy against the head of my cock, her legs instinctively wrapping around me.

"Hunter—" she starts, voice hoarse and breathless.

I thrust upward before she can finish, burying myself inside her in one savage stroke. The sensation is indescribable as her wet heat envelops me completely. A guttural sound rips from my chest, something between a growl and a groan as I finally feel her pussy stretched around my cock.

"Fuck," I hiss, my forehead dropping to rest against hers. "Fucking perfect."

The relief is overwhelming, like quenching a thirst I've had for eternity. Her walls pulse around me, still sensitive from her orgasm, gripping me like she was made for this—made for me.

I hold her suspended against the tree, her pussy stretched tight around me, savoring the way her body trembles. My cock throbs inside her, every pulse a claim of ownership.

"You feel that?" I growl, withdrawing almost completely before slamming back in. "That's your cunt surrendering. Fighting me with your mouth while your pussy begs for more."

Her nails dig into my shoulders, drawing blood as I establish a punishing rhythm. Each thrust drives her harder against the rough bark, the pain of it mixing with pleasure in those little sounds escaping her throat.

"I knew from the moment I saw you on that cliff," I rasp, driving deeper. "Standing in the rain like some fucking storm goddess. I knew I'd have you just like this, taking my cock while you pretend you don't want it."

The slick sound of her wetness fills the night air as I pound into her relentlessly. Her head falls back, exposing her throat, and I latch onto it, sucking hard enough to leave marks Olivia will question tomorrow.

"Your sister's planning our fucking wedding," I snarl against her throat, "picking out china patterns while I mark her sister's body with my teeth."

Her walls clench violently around me at those words, betraying how the wrongness of it all turns her on.

"That's it," I hiss, "squeeze that pretty cunt around me. Show me how much you love being your sister's fiancé's dirty secret."

I shift my angle, hitting deeper, making her gasp with each thrust. The wild sounds she makes drive me to a frenzy.

"When I sit at your family dinner table," I pant, sweat dripping down my spine, "I'll be thinking about your pussy stretched around my cock in the fucking woods."

She's sobbing now, pleasure-pain tears streaming down her face as I consume her. I capture that broken sound with my mouth, kissing her viciously, my tongue conquering hers while my cock continues its relentless invasion below.

"Your cunt belongs to me now," I whisper against her lips, voice dropping to something dark and possessive. "Mine to fill. Mine to fuck. Mine to ruin for any other man."

Her body tightens around me as another orgasm builds. Something shifts in her expression—the conflict becoming unbearable.

"I can't be yours," Aurora gasps, her voice cracking as I continue to thrust into her. "Not while you're engaged to her. I can't."

Her words hit me harder than they should. I slow my movements, still buried deep inside her, and catch her tear-streaked face between my hands. Now, her chest is heaving with more than just physical exertion.

"Look at me," I command, gentler than before.

Her azure eyes meet mine, filled with shame and desire in equal measure. A sensation I've never experienced before twists my chest. This isn't just about possession anymore.

"Listen to me, Aurora," I say, my voice dropping to a harsh whisper. "I have no intention of ever marrying your sister."

I punctuate my words with a slow, deep thrust that makes her gasp.

"The engagement is business. A fucking merger. It won't be long before it's over."

Her eyes search mine, looking for deception; she won't find it. In this moment, with her wrapped around me, I've never been more certain of anything.

"The only thing I want is you," I tell her, the admission torn from somewhere I didn't know existed. "Only you."

I capture her mouth again, swallowing whatever protest might follow. I don't want to hear doubt or hesitation. There's only this. Her body taking mine, her tears on my tongue, the impossible thing growing between us that I can't name but refuse to deny.

17

AURORA

"The only thing I want is you. Only you."

His words slam through me with more force than his body, lighting up something primitive inside me. Something I've been fighting since I first saw him on that cliff edge.

"Hunter..." His name falls from my lips like a prayer, a surrender.

My body responds before my mind can catch up, inner muscles clenching around his thickness as a wave of pleasure crashes over me. The realization that this powerful, dangerous man wants only me pushes me over the edge.

"That's it," he growls, his voice dropping to something barely human. "Coming on my cock just from hearing you're the only one I want."

My vision blurs as the orgasm tears through me, muscles spasming uncontrollably around his impossible girth. He doesn't stop, doesn't slow, driving deeper as I shatter.

"Look at you," he snarls against my throat, teeth

grazing my pulse. "Wild thing pretending to be civilized until I stripped it all away."

His hips snap against mine, the base of his cock grinding against my clit with each thrust, prolonging my release until I can barely breathe.

"Feel how fucking perfect you take me?" His words are hot against my ear, his breath coming in harsh pants. "Like your cunt was made to grip me."

I'm whimpering now, overwhelmed, clawing at his shoulders while he consumes me. My body no longer feels like my own. It feels like it belongs to this moment, to him, to whatever dark magic exists between us.

"My perfect fucking match," he continues, each word punctuated by a brutal thrust. "My good girl with claws and teeth, fighting me even as you come apart."

His hand slides up to tangle in my hair, yanking my head back to expose my throat. He bites down on the tender skin, not quite breaking it, marking me.

"Mine," he growls against the bruise forming on my skin. "Say it. Tell me who owns this sweet cunt that's dripping for me."

"You." The word tears from my throat. "You own it. You own me."

His eyes flash with triumph, and I can't stand it anymore. I surge forward, capturing his mouth with mine, kissing him with every ounce of desperation I've been drowning in. My teeth clash against his, my tongue seeking entrance, tasting myself on his lips.

"I've wanted you since that day on the cliff," I confess against his mouth, the words spilling out like blood from a wound. "When you pulled me back from the edge. Something in me recognized something in you."

His grip tightens, possessive and fierce, as if he's afraid I might vanish.

"God, I hated hearing you were engaged to Olivia. It felt like someone had reached inside and crushed my heart." My voice breaks. "I told myself it was just because I didn't want her to be with someone like you, but it was a lie. I couldn't stand the thought of you touching her instead of me."

In one fluid motion, he withdraws from me and carries me away from the tree to lay me on my back on the damp earth. The cool ground presses against my heated skin as he pins my wrists above my head with one large hand.

"Say it again," he demands, knee nudging my thighs apart. "Tell me who you belong to while I fuck you into the ground."

"You," I gasp as he enters me again, harder this time, the new angle making me arch off the dirt. "I'm yours, Hunter."

He growls, the sound vibrating through his chest and into mine. His free hand grips my hip hard enough to bruise as he pounds into me. The force of his thrusts pushes me against the earth, grass, and soil, scratching my back.

I'm beyond caring, beyond thinking. My legs wrap around his waist, heels digging into his lower back, urging him deeper. My nails rake down his arms when he releases my wrists, leaving red trails on his skin.

We're animals now, rutting in the dirt beneath the stars, his teeth at my throat, my cries echoing through the garden.

Stars blur above me as Hunter's pace becomes frantic, almost punishing. His movements grow more possessive with each thrust, like he's trying to claim every inch of me.

The weight of his body pins me to the earth as if he's determined to fuse us together.

"Fuck," he growls against my throat, his voice ragged and raw. "You feel too good. So perfect around my cock."

I arch beneath him, meeting each savage thrust, my body no longer my own but something wild and unfamiliar. Something that belongs to him.

"I should fill you up," he groans, his rhythm faltering. "Put a baby in you. Watch you swell with my child."

The words shock through me like lightning, jolting me momentarily from the haze of pleasure. "I'm on birth control," I gasp, the words tumbling out instinctively.

Hunter's eyes lock onto mine, something ancient and possessive darkening them. His hand finds my throat, thumb pressing against my pulse as his hips slam against mine with renewed purpose.

"Not for long," he snarls, the words vibrating against my skin. "I want to breed you, Aurora. Want to see you grow round with my child."

The need in his voice makes me shiver. There's no negotiation in his tone, just absolute certainty. Like my body is a territory he's already claimed, my future is already decided.

"I want to mark you from the inside out," he continues, each word punctuated by a brutal thrust. "Want everyone to see who you belong to. My seed. My child. Mine."

His possessiveness should terrify me, but instead, it sends another wave of heat coursing through me. Some instinctive part of me responds to his claiming, my body tightening around him as if eager to accept what he's offering.

His words ignite something primitive in me, something I never knew existed. Every cell in my body vibrates with need as his cock fills me, stretching me to my limits.

"You like that idea," he growls, not a question but a statement of fact. "Your cunt just got tighter. So fucking wet thinking about me knocking you up."

I can't deny it. My body responds to his filthy promises with shameless hunger. My nails dig deeper into his shoulders as I arch against him, seeking more, needing everything.

"Please," I beg, not even recognizing my own voice anymore. "Please, Hunter."

His laugh is dark against my throat. "Please, what, sweetheart? Please fill you up? Please make you mine forever?"

"Yes," I gasp as he hits something deep inside me that makes my vision blur. "God, yes."

He shifts suddenly, flipping onto his back and pulling me on top of him. The new position drives him impossibly deeper, and I cry out, my hands bracing against his chest.

"You think you're in control now?" he taunts, his fingers digging into my hips. "Ride my cock, baby. Show me how badly you want it."

I move desperately, grinding down on him, chasing the pleasure building inside me. His eyes devour me, hungry and possessive.

"That's it," he praises, voice rough. "Look at you. So fucking beautiful taking what you need from me." His thumb finds my clit, circling roughly. "But know this isn't just about pleasure. This is about power."

My rhythm falters as his words register through my haze of lust.

"Every time you think you're free of me," he continues, voice dropping to something sinister yet seductive, "you'll remember this—how perfectly we fit together. How I'm the only one who sees the darkness inside you and loves it."

That unexpected tenderness wrapped in dominance sends me careening toward the edge.

"And I do love it," he whispers, his eyes boring into mine with unexpected vulnerability. "Everything about you. The light and the shadow. Mine to protect. Mine to possess."

"Show me how good you can be," Hunter demands, his voice commanding as he grips my hips. "Milk my cock with that tight pussy. Make yourself come for me like a good girl."

The way he says it, it sounds half like a command, and half like worship, making me shudder above him. I roll my hips, feeling him stretch me impossibly wide. His cock hits places inside me I never knew existed.

"That's it," he growls. "Squeeze that pretty cunt around me. Show me how badly you want to please me."

I clench around him deliberately, watching his eyes darken with pleasure. The power I feel is intoxicating, having this dangerous man at my mercy, even as he commands me.

"I want to be good for you," I whisper, the confession tearing from somewhere deep and hidden. "So good."

His thumb finds my clit, circling with just the right pressure. "Then come for me. Now."

My body responds instantly, like he's found some secret control switch inside me. Pleasure explodes outward from where we're joined, radiating through my limbs as I grind down harder.

"That's my good girl," he praises as I shatter above him. "Taking what you need, giving me what I want."

I lose myself in the sensation, riding him through my orgasm, muscles clenching rhythmically around his thickness. I'm whimpering his name, over and over, as my body obeys his command perfectly.

"Keep going," he orders through gritted teeth. "Don't stop until I tell you."

I continue moving, milking his cock with deliberate pulses of my inner muscles, watching his face contort with pleasure. Despite my exhaustion, I want nothing more than to please him, to be exactly what he demands.

"Such a good girl for me," he groans, his hands guiding my hips in the rhythm he craves. "My perfect little slut."

"I'm going to breed this tight little cunt," Hunter growls, flipping me beneath him again and pinning my wrists above my head. "Going to fill you with my cum until it's dripping down your thighs."

I arch beneath him, offering myself like a sacrifice.

"You want that, don't you?" He thrusts harder, the sound of our bodies slapping together echoing through the night air. "Want me to pump you full, make your belly swell with my seed."

"Yes," I gasp, my legs wrapping tighter around his waist. "God, yes."

His pace grows punishing, each thrust bottoming out inside me. "Say it properly. Tell me what you want."

"I want you to breed me," I moan, the words feeling filthy and perfect on my tongue. "Fill me up. Make me yours."

Hunter's eyes flash with possession. "That's it. Beg for my cum."

The degradation makes me clench around him, my body betraying how much his words affect me. He notices immediately.

"You love this, don't you? Being fucked like an animal in the dirt, begging to be bred." His hand finds my throat, applying just enough pressure to make my head swim. "Say it. Tell me how much you want my cum deep inside you."

"Please," I whimper, my nails digging into his shoulders. "I need it. Need you to fill me up."

His teeth find my earlobe, biting down as he drives deeper. "Your body was made for taking my cock, for carrying my child."

The filthy words push me over the edge again, my body convulsing around him as another orgasm tears through me. I cry out his name, back arching off the ground as pleasure consumes me.

"That's right," he praises darkly. "Squeeze my cock with that tight pussy. Milk every drop from me when I flood your womb."

His words about breeding me, making me swell with his child, should terrify me. Even knowing my birth control will prevent any consequences, the fantasy of it—of being claimed so completely, so permanently—sends electric currents of pleasure through every nerve.

"You're mine," Hunter growls against my throat, his thrusts becoming erratic, more desperate. "Every. Fucking. Inch."

I dig my fingers into his back, feeling the muscles tense under my touch as he approaches his climax. "Yes," I gasp, arching into him. "Yours."

His breath comes in harsh pants against my skin. "Going to fill you up," he snarls, his voice barely human. "Mark you from the inside."

"Do it," I beg, wrapping my legs tighter around him, pulling him deeper. "Please, Hunter."

His rhythm falters, his body tensing above mine. With a guttural sound that's more animal than man, his teeth find the junction where my neck meets my shoulder. He bites down, not quite breaking skin, but hard enough to bruise as his hips jerk against mine.

The sharp pain of his teeth contrasts with the hot pulse of him emptying inside me. The twin sensations of pain and pleasure, and taking and giving, spiral together, igniting another orgasm that tears through me without warning. I cry out, my body convulsing around him as he continues to fill me, the pain from his bite intensifying every wave of pleasure.

My vision blurs at the edges, my entire existence narrowed to the points where our bodies connect. His teeth on my flesh, his cock pulsing inside me, his cum marking me in a way no one else ever has.

The waves of pleasure finally begin to recede, my body trembling with aftershocks as reality crashes back. My sister's face flashes through my mind—Olivia's bright smile, her excited chatter about wedding plans, the way she looked at Hunter with stars in her eyes.

Oh god. What have I done?

"I need to go," I gasp, suddenly aware of the dirt pressing into my back, the cool night air against my exposed skin, the sticky evidence of what we've done between my thighs. I push against Hunter's chest, trying to scramble out from under him. "This was a mistake. I can't. Olivia—"

Hunter's hands capture my wrists, pinning them firmly on either side of my head. His weight presses me deeper into the earth, immobilizing me beneath him. His eyes, so recently clouded with pleasure, are now sharp and uncompromising.

"No time for a conscience now, sweetheart," he growls, his thumb brushing across my lower lip. "You're mine until the sun comes up. I'm going to fuck you all night."

"But my sister—" My voice breaks on the words.

"Is not here." He cuts me off, his tone brooking no argument. "It's just you and me now. Just us and what we both want." His lips ghost across my jaw to my ear. "And we both know what you want, don't we? No matter how guilty it makes you feel after."

His body shifts against mine, his hardness already returning against my thigh. "The time for thinking is over," he whispers, teeth grazing my earlobe. "I'm not letting you go until I've had my fill."

I should fight harder. I should scream. I should make him understand what this will do to Olivia. But instead, I feel my resistance melting under his touch as his mouth claims mine again.

18

HUNTER

I stretch out across Aurora's bed, my muscles pleasantly sore as sunlight filters through half-drawn curtains. My hand reaches across the sheets, finding them cool to the touch. Empty.

Cracking my neck, I scan the room. No sign of her. The bathroom door stands open, darkness beyond. Her scent lingers everywhere—on the pillows, the sheets, my skin.

I haven't felt this completely drained yet utterly satisfied in my entire life. Last night was... fucking transcendent.

After taking her against that tree and in the dirt, I carried her back to the house, her legs still wrapped around my waist, my cock still buried inside her. We barely made it through the door before I had her pressed against the wall, driving into her until she came screaming my name again.

We left a trail of destruction through the house. The dining table where I bent her over and feasted on her from behind until her legs gave out. The stairs where she took me in her mouth, looking up with those defiant blue eyes as I fisted her hair. The shower where I pinned her hands above her head and made her beg.

And finally, this bed, where I broke her down completely and rebuilt her as mine.

I lost count of how many times she came. The way she'd whimper and tighten around me, her body convulsing, tears streaming down her face from the intensity. I became addicted to forcing those reactions from her repeatedly.

"Never enough," I'd growled in her ear as dawn approached, sliding down her body to taste her again, lapping at her oversensitive flesh until she sobbed with pleasure. "I'm going to make you come until you forget your own name."

And I did. By the end, she could barely form coherent sentences, just pleading moans and my name on her lips.

But now she's gone.

I sit up, running a hand through my hair. The clock on the bedside table reads 9:38 AM.

I get out of bed, somewhat annoyed she's not still lying beside me. My clothes are scattered across the bedroom floor. I pull on my pants, not bothering with underwear, and slip my shirt over my shoulders without buttoning it. I don't bother with socks and step into my shoes.

The house is quiet as I move through the hallway. Last night, these walls echoed with her screams of pleasure. Now there's nothing but silence.

I find her in the kitchen, perched on a stool at the island counter, clutching a coffee mug like it's a shield. Her hair is pulled back in a messy bun, her eyes puffy, and her lips still swollen from my kisses. She's wearing an oversized sweater that slips off one shoulder, revealing the marks I left on her neck.

When she sees me, her entire body tenses. No smile. No good morning. Just a flash of something that looks like regret in those blue eyes.

"You need to leave." Her voice is flat, emotionless. "Martha will be here in twenty minutes."

I lean against the doorframe, studying her. "We need to talk, Aurora."

"There's nothing to talk about." She stands, putting the island between us. "Last night was... it shouldn't have happened. You're engaged to my sister."

"I told you that's a business arrangement, a temporary one."

"It doesn't matter what you call it." She clutches her mug tighter. "Please, just go."

I push off from the doorframe and cross the kitchen in three strides. "We're talking about this."

Her eyes widen as I approach, but she doesn't back away. "Hunter, don't—"

"Don't what?" I step closer until I'm towering over her. "Don't remind me how many times you came screaming my name last night? Don't point out how your body knows it's master every time I'm near?"

Her eyes narrow, a flash of defiance cutting through the guilt. "And how exactly would this work, Hunter? What's your grand plan?" Aurora sets her mug down with enough force that coffee sloshes over the rim. "Do I just tell Olivia I fucked her fiancé? *Sorry, sis, I know you're planning your wedding, but I've been sleeping with the groom?*"

I almost smile at her fire. Even cornered, she's magnificent.

"You don't tell her anything," I say simply. "That's my responsibility."

"Your responsibility?" She laughs bitterly. "And what will you say? How do you imagine this plays out where my sister doesn't hate me for the rest of our lives?"

I move closer, trapping her against the counter. "Olivia

will be disappointed the engagement didn't work out, but she'll recover. People break engagements every day."

"But not like this! Not with their sister!"

"Olivia doesn't need to know about us right away." I trace a finger along her collarbone where my mark blooms purple against her skin. "I'll end things with her. Business differences with your father, incompatible goals, whatever makes it clear. After a reasonable period, we can be seen together."

"You think it's that simple?" Aurora pushes against my chest, but I don't budge. "My sister will figure it out. She's not stupid."

"I never said she was. But by the time she does, it won't matter. She'll have moved on."

Aurora shakes her head, tears gathering in her eyes. "You don't understand what you're asking. She's my sister. The only family I have left other than my stepdad, and he'd freak out too."

I reach out, capturing her chin between my thumb and forefinger. "I don't care."

Her eyes widen. "What?"

"I don't care about Olivia, your father, or anyone else who might object." I hold her gaze, letting her see the truth in my eyes. "I'll be your new family, Aurora. The only one that matters."

She starts to shake her head, but I continue before she can argue.

"You can fight this all you want, but in the end, you'll accept your fate." I soften my grip, trailing my fingers down her neck. "Until then, I'll give you space. Time to come to terms with what's happening between us."

Tears glisten in her eyes, but there's something else

there too—desire, need, the same hunger that's consuming me.

When I lower my mouth to hers, she doesn't pull away. Her lips part instantly, and what begins as a claiming turns desperate, needy. To my surprise, Aurora kisses back with equal fervor, her fingers digging into my shoulders as she presses herself against me.

She wants this as badly as I do.

I lift her onto the counter, stepping between her legs as her hands slide into my hair. She moans into my mouth, and the sound nearly breaks my control.

The crunch of tires on gravel cuts through the moment.

"Shit," Aurora gasps, yanking her mouth from mine. "Martha's early." She pushes at my chest, panic replacing desire in her eyes. "You need to go. Please use the side entrance by the pantry. She can't see you here."

I can't help but smirk. "Only a dirty little secret for you and you alone, hmm?"

She glares, but there's no real heat behind it. "Hunter, please."

I steal one more kiss, deep and claiming, feeling her momentary surrender before I pull away. "This isn't over."

I turn and stride down the hallway toward the side door, slipping through it just as I hear the front door open and Martha's cheerful greeting echo through the house.

19

AURORA

I drag myself through the door of our apartment, exhausted both physically and emotionally. The memory of Hunter's hands on me, his mouth against mine, haunts every step. Even now, hours later, my body aches in ways that remind me exactly what we did last night. What I let him do to me. What I wanted him to do.

My sister's fiancé.

The apartment buzzes with activity before I even close the door. Music plays from Olivia's room, and I hear her singing along, something upbeat and cheerful that makes my stomach twist with dread.

"Liv?" I call out, dropping my bag by the door.

"Aurora!" Olivia appears in the hallway, practically bouncing. "You're finally home! Where have you been? I thought you'd be back from Portland yesterday!"

I force a smile, guilt crawling up my throat like bile. "Sorry, I took a detour at Dad's place. Needed some time to think."

"Well, you picked the worst time to disappear!" She grabs my hand, pulling me toward her bedroom. "Look!"

Her room looks like a fashion bomb exploded. Clothes cover every surface, and a massive suitcase sits open on the bed, already half-filled with designer outfits.

"What's happening?" I ask, though part of me already knows. Hunter's doing.

"I got invited to London Fashion Week! Can you believe it?" Olivia twirls, her face radiant with excitement. "Front row seats to all the major shows, exclusive parties, the works!"

My heart sinks. "That's... amazing, Liv. But what about the wedding? Isn't it in a few weeks?"

"That's the best part!" She grabs another dress from her closet. "I called Hunter right away, worried he'd be upset about me taking off so close to the wedding, but he was completely supportive! Said I absolutely had to take this opportunity, that we can handle any wedding details when I get back."

Every word is a knife. I picture Hunter on the phone with her, encouraging her to leave while plotting our next encounter.

"He's so understanding," Olivia continues, oblivious to my turmoil. "I honestly thought he might be annoyed, but he insisted I go. Isn't that sweet of him?"

I nod, not trusting my voice. Sweet isn't the word I'd use. Strategic. My fingers curl into fists as I realize he's deliberately getting her out of the way.

"When do you leave?" I manage to ask.

"Tomorrow morning! I know it's last-minute, but apparently someone dropped out, and they offered me their spot." She holds up two pairs of shoes. "Which ones?"

"The strappy ones," I say, pointing to the silver heels. "They go with everything."

Olivia beams, tossing them into her suitcase. "You're right. Perfect for the afterparties."

I perch on the edge of her bed, picking at a loose thread on her comforter. "So... you and Hunter. This trip doesn't bother him at all?"

She shrugs, folding a silk blouse. "Honestly, we barely know each other. It's not like we're some love match."

"What do you mean?" I ask, though I already know the answer. I need to hear her say it.

"Come on." Olivia rolls her eyes. "Dad arranged this whole thing. Hunter needed stability for his company, and Dad wanted connections to Hunter's tech empire. It's a business arrangement wrapped in a white dress." She pauses, frowning. "We've never even been on a proper date. Just business dinners with Dad present."

My stomach twists. "You're marrying someone you've never even kissed?"

"Welcome to high society," she says with a theatrical sigh. "Dad says we'll develop feelings later. Hunter's attractive enough, and we're compatible on paper. The rest will follow."

I watch her pack so casually, talking about marrying a man she doesn't know—a man who spent last night doing unimaginable things to her sister.

"Doesn't that bother you?" I ask, my voice smaller than I intended.

Olivia stops folding, considering the question. "Sometimes. But I grew up knowing this was likely. Dad always said marriage at our level is about strategic partnerships first." She smiles, but it doesn't reach her eyes. "At least Hunter is gorgeous and not some sixty-year-old oil baron."

"But don't you want love?" The question burns in my throat.

"Maybe we'll fall in love eventually." She zips a cosmetics bag. "Or maybe we'll have a cordial partnership and separate lives. Either way, the Harrison-Reed merger happens."

Merger. That's all it is to her. All it is to our father. A business transaction.

But to Hunter... to me... It's something else entirely.

I swallow hard, fidgeting with the comforter. "What if... what if the wedding didn't happen for some reason? Would you be upset?"

Olivia pauses, a designer dress hanging from her fingertips, and shrugs. "Honestly? Not really. Hunter's a catch, but so are dozens of others in our circle. I'd find someone else." She tosses the dress into her suitcase. "As long as he's rich and Dad approves, I don't particularly care who I marry."

Her words hit me like a slap. I've always known Olivia lives in a different world than I do. One of social media followers and surface-level connections, but hearing her reduce marriage to a financial transaction makes my chest ache.

"That's... practical," I manage.

"That's life." She flashes a bright smile, utterly unbothered. "We can't all be romantics like you, waiting for some grand love story."

I look away, remembering how Mom used to look at Dad before everything fell apart. Their eyes would speak volumes across dinner tables. The way they danced in the kitchen when they thought no one was watching. The little notes he'd leave in her purse.

"I saw what my mom and dad had," I say quietly. "Before... everything. They were so in love."

Olivia rolls her eyes. "And look how that turned out."

The words sting because they echo my deepest fears. I remember finding Mom crying in the bathroom after Dad died. Her hollow eyes staring at old photographs. The way grief consumed her so completely that even cancer couldn't compete with it.

"That's the problem with love," I say. "When it's real, losing it destroys you."

"Exactly why I'm not interested," Olivia says, piling jewelry into a travel case. "No one can break your heart if you don't give it away in the first place."

I nod, but something in me rebels against her cynicism. Despite everything I've seen, despite the fear that's kept me from serious relationships, I've never been able to make myself that detached.

Olivia's casual dismissal of marriage strikes something in me. Maybe... maybe there's a way out of this moral nightmare. If she truly doesn't care about Hunter beyond what he brings to the family business, could I possibly talk to her about my feelings for him? Would she understand that what Hunter and I share is more than just physical attraction?

"Liv," I start cautiously, "what if someone else was interested in Hunter? Someone who actually had genuine feelings for him?"

She laughs as she sorts through her accessories. "They'd be welcome to the emotional labor. As long as the business partnership stays intact, I couldn't care less who he sleeps with after we're married."

My heart races. This might be easier than I thought. I take a deep breath, preparing to confess everything.

"Actually, I wanted to talk to you about—"

A knock at the door cuts me off. I hear our housekeeper, Maria, and familiar laughter that freezes me.

"Ms. Olivia? Your friends are here."

Olivia squeals with delight, abandoning her packing to rush to the door. I follow more slowly, my confession dying in my throat as Chloe, Daisy, and Grace spill into our apartment, carrying overnight bags and bottles of champagne.

"Surprise!" Chloe yells, her voice echoing through the apartment as she tosses her leopard-print duffel onto the couch.

"What are you all doing here?" I ask, forcing a smile while panic blooms in my chest.

Daisy gives me a knowing look before hugging Olivia. "Your sister invited us for an impromptu packing party and sleepover before she jets off to London."

"I figured we needed one last girls' night before fashion week," Olivia explains, taking a champagne bottle from Grace. "Plus, I needed fashion consultants I actually trust."

Grace approaches me, her eyes searching mine. "You okay? You look like you've seen a ghost."

"I'm fine," I lie, watching as Chloe and Olivia head toward the kitchen for glasses. "Just tired."

Daisy joins us, speaking in a hushed tone. "Did you tell her yet?"

I shake my head minutely, my opportunity slipping away with every passing second. Whatever confession I was about to make will have to wait.

20

HUNTER

I stand in the shadowy expanse of the Vipers' underground headquarters, watching as five hooded figures kneel before Jax King. The chamber's dim lighting catches on Jax's silver rings as he moves between the recruits, his presence commanding absolute silence from the thirty assembled members.

"Your trials have proven your worth," Jax announces, his voice carrying through the cavernous space without effort. "Tonight, you cease to be individuals. Tonight, you become part of something greater."

I nod at appropriate moments, maintaining the appearance of attentiveness. Inside my head, I'm replaying Aurora pinned against that tree, her skin flushed as she came apart for me. The memory of her taste lingers on my tongue.

Penn catches my eye from across the circle and raises an eyebrow. I straighten my posture, refocusing on Jax as he presents each recruit with their Viper insignia.

"These five survived when others failed," Jax continues. "Remember. We are not friends. We are not family. We are power incarnate."

The assembly repeats the mantra in perfect unison. I join them, the words automatic after fifteen years.

My thoughts drift to Olivia Harrison. The engagement must end without alienating her father. Derek's shipping infrastructure is too valuable to lose over something as trivial as his daughter's feelings. Perhaps an indiscretion on Olivia's part—something I could arrange through Ari's connections. Or better yet, a gentle redirection of her interests.

Jax's eyes lock with mine briefly. I've known him long enough to recognize the warning there. Nothing escapes his notice.

"Hunter Reed," he calls. "Present the final mark."

I move forward automatically, removing the branding iron from the glowing coals. The emblem glows orange white in the darkness. The first recruit's scream echoes against the stone walls as I press it to his shoulder.

All I can think about is how Aurora's body felt against mine, and how soon I can have her again.

Jax steps forward as the last recruit's branding sizzles to completion. The acrid scent of burned flesh hangs in the air. I return the iron to the coals and take my place in the inner circle.

"Now that our ranks are replenished," Jax says, his voice deceptively soft, "it's time our newest members understand exactly what they've joined."

He moves to the center of the chamber and taps a panel on the floor. A holographic display illuminates the space, showing a network of connections spanning the entire city.

"The Vipers began as a simple pact between old money families," Jax explains, indicating the core nodes on the display. "A mutual agreement to protect our interests when the law proved... inconvenient."

The display shifts, expanding outward like a spider's web.

"Today, we control seventeen judges on the federal bench." Red dots illuminate across the city map. "Twenty-six politicians, including the mayor and three state senators." More lights blink on. "Forty-two police captains and the police commissioner himself."

I watch the newest members' faces. The reality of what they've joined is finally sinking in.

"Our corporate division," Jax continues, nodding toward Blaine, "has executed hostile takeovers of fourteen major companies in the last decade alone. We control real estate, banking, tech, and medical infrastructure."

Penn chuckles beside me as one recruit visibly pales.

"And the streets?" Jax gestures to Grayson. "Every drug dealer, every pimp, every gang leader answers to us or disappears. We decide who thrives and who dies."

The hologram expands to show the entire city grid, now a constellation of Viper control points.

"What began as protection has evolved into governance," Jax says. "The people believe they elect their leaders. They're wrong. We are the true power. The shadow government that rules from darkness."

He closes the display with a wave of his hand. "Remember this when you're tempted to question orders or pursue personal vendettas. We are not individuals. We are the system itself."

The five recruits rise from their knees as Jax beckons them to the center of the chamber. Hansen catches my eye, his face betraying nothing. Smart man. His composure during the claustrophobia test impressed me, though I'd never admit it aloud.

"Blood binds deeper than any contract," Jax announces,

removing an obsidian dagger from his jacket. The blade gleams under the chamber's lights. "What we create tonight cannot be undone."

He slices across his palm without flinching, letting the blood pool in a silver chalice held by Blaine.

"I lead not through birthright but through strength and vision. My blood carries that promise."

Each founding member follows suit. When my turn comes, I drag the blade across my flesh, watching crimson well up from the cut. The pain barely registers.

"Drink," Jax commands when the chalice reaches Hansen, "and become bound to us for eternity."

Hansen hesitates only momentarily before bringing the cup to his lips. The other four recruits follow his example, each drinking.

"Your oath is sealed," Jax says, moving to a control panel. "But words and blood mean nothing without understanding consequences."

The chamber's lights dim as a projection appears on the far wall. I recognize the footage immediately and fight to keep my expression neutral.

"Dominic Hughes. Former congressman. Former Viper." Jax's voice cuts through the darkness as the video shows Dominic strapped to a medical table, screaming soundlessly. "He voted against our interests, believing his political connections would save him."

The footage shifts to show the aftermath. What remained of Dominic barely resembled a human.

"Aaron Michaels shared our methods with federal agents." Another video plays, this one more graphic than the last. "His betrayal cost us three operations and millions in revenue."

Several recruits visibly pale as the footage continues,

showing five more examples of traitors' fates. Hansen's eyes remain fixed on the screen, his jaw clenched tight.

"Loyalty is our one absolute," Jax says, turning off the projection. "Break your vow, and you pray for the mercy of a quick death. There are no second chances."

Throughout the ceremony, I catch Jax's eyes on me more than usual. Not his typical supervisory glance, but something more penetrating. I maintain my composure, but the weight of his stare becomes increasingly difficult to ignore.

As the recruits disperse and the chamber empties, Jax appears at my side. His hand clamps firmly on my shoulder.

"A word, Hunter." Not a request.

He guides me to a private alcove where the surveillance cameras have conveniently malfunctioned for years. Our personal dead zone for conversations that need to stay buried.

"The Harrison situation," he says without preamble. "It's becoming a distraction."

My pulse quickens, though my face remains impassive. "The merger with Harrison Industries is progressing as planned. Derek will sign next month."

Jax's smile doesn't reach his eyes. "I'm not referring to Derek or his shipping empire."

Fuck.

"Aurora Harrison," he continues. "Quite the fascinating woman, from what I understand. Smart. Beautiful. Her sister's fiancée's obsession."

I feel a chill despite the underground chamber's warmth. "You're monitoring me."

"I monitor everything that threatens our interests." Jax steps closer, his voice dropping. "Your engagement to Olivia secures Derek's cooperation. Now you're risking it for what? A few nights with the stepsister?"

"I know what I'm doing," I reply, my tone sharper than intended.

"Do you?" Jax looks genuinely curious. "Because from where I stand, you're letting your cock make decisions your brain should be handling."

"The engagement was temporary. I'll end it without compromising Derek's deal."

Jax's laugh is hollow. "And if he takes exception to you fucking his stepdaughter while discarding his true heir? Family men can be unpredictable when their children are involved."

"I've calculated the risk."

"Your personal desires," Jax states, "must never compromise this organization. We've sacrificed too much to let one man's obsession destroy what we've built."

As he walks away, I'm left wondering exactly how much he knows. The cliff. The garden. The night at her house. Are there cameras I missed? People reporting back to him?

Or worse, is Aurora herself compromised?

21

AURORA

The elevator ride to Hunter's penthouse feels like ascending to my own execution. Each floor ticks by with the steady rhythm of a countdown, my reflection in the polished brass doors showing a woman I barely recognize with haunted eyes and rigid posture.

I shouldn't be here. I should have called instead. But some conversations need to happen face-to-face.

My phone buzzes with another text from Olivia, sending photos from London Fashion Week. My stomach twists with guilt. I couldn't tell her before she left. The words formed in my throat but died before reaching my lips.

"The worst part about guilt is how it eats you from the inside," my mom once told me. She was right. I haven't slept properly since that night with Hunter, since I betrayed my sister in the most fundamental way possible.

The elevator doors slide open to reveal Hunter's private foyer. The penthouse sprawls before me with sleek lines and floor-to-ceiling windows overlooking the city. Beautiful and cold, just like its owner.

I step inside without announcing myself. He'll know I'm here. He always seems to know exactly where I am.

"You need to stop sending me messages," I say into the apparent emptiness of the apartment. "This, whatever this is, it's over."

My voice sounds stronger than I feel. Good. I need that strength now.

"I mean it, Hunter. I can't do this to Olivia. She's my sister."

Movement catches my eye as Hunter emerges from his home office. He's barefoot, dressed in black pants and an unbuttoned shirt that reveals the muscled torso I've tried and failed to forget.

"Aurora." My name on his lips sounds like both a prayer and a curse. "I wondered how long it would take you to come."

"I'm not here for that." I clench my fists at my sides. "I'm here to end it."

His eyes never leave mine as he approaches, each step deliberate. "Are you?"

My heart hammers against my ribs. Ending things with Hunter should be simple. He's engaged to my sister, for god's sake, but nothing about him has ever been simple.

"Why are you really here, Aurora?" Hunter's voice turns cold, the warmth I'd glimpsed moments ago vanishing like it never existed.

"I told you. I'm ending this." My resolve strengthens with each word. "Whatever happened between us was a mistake."

A humorless smile plays across his lips. "A mistake? Is that what you call it when you screamed my name? When your nails left marks down my back?"

"Stop it."

"Or how about when you begged me not to stop?" His eyes gleam with cruel amusement. "That's quite a mistake."

The distance between us feels electric. I take a step back, needing physical space from his presence.

"You can joke all you want, but I'm serious. I won't continue this while you're engaged to my sister."

Hunter circles me slowly, predatory. "We both know Olivia doesn't care about me."

"That doesn't matter," I counter, holding my ground despite the intensity of his gaze. "She's still my sister. Our relationship means everything to me. I won't destroy that, not even for..." I gesture helplessly between us.

"For the best sex of your life?" he finishes, his voice dropping an octave.

Heat floods my face. "This isn't about sex."

"No?" He steps closer. "Then why can't you look me in the eye when you say you want to end things?"

I force myself to meet his gaze. "I'm serious, Hunter."

"And yet you came here, to my home, instead of calling." His fingers brush my cheek. "Interesting choice for someone ending things."

I jerk away from his touch. "Olivia may not love you, but she's my sister. I won't betray her like this."

Hunter's laugh is sharp, dangerous. "Olivia's convenient trip to London wasn't a coincidence, Aurora. I arranged it and convinced her father it would be good publicity before the engagement party and suggested which designers she should see."

My stomach drops. While I suspected he might have orchestrated it, I didn't really want to believe it. "What?"

"I orchestrated everything. Right down to the exact dates she'd be gone." His smile is triumphant. "I create the circumstances I need. Always."

Despite already knowing he was behind her invite and trip, I glare at him. "You manipulated everything just to get what you want."

"I always get what I want." A predatory gleam lights his eyes. "And I want you."

Fury surges through me. "You're a monster."

"Perhaps." He steps closer. "But I'm the monster you crave."

"Go to hell." I push past him, but his hand catches my wrist, spinning me back.

"Tell me you don't want this," he challenges, his face inches from mine. "Tell me, and I'll let you walk out that door."

Words fail me as his proximity overwhelms my senses. The scent of his cologne make me dizzy.

"I—I don't..." My protest dies as his thumb traces circles on the inside of my wrist.

"Liar."

His lips crash against mine, and whatever resistance I had crumbles instantly. My hands fist in his shirt, simultaneously pushing and pulling. I bite his lower lip hard enough to taste blood.

Hunter growls against my mouth. "There she is."

He lifts me without warning, my back slamming against the wall as my legs instinctively wrap around his waist. My dress rides up my thighs as his hands grip my ass, fingers digging into my flesh.

"Tell me to stop," he demands, voice ragged. "Tell me you don't want this."

Instead of answering, I pull his shirt off his shoulders.

My nails rake down his chest, leaving angry red trails in their wake. His eyes darken with savage pleasure.

"I hate what you do to me," I gasp as his teeth graze my neck.

"No, you hate how much you love it." His hand slides between us, pushing my panties aside. When his fingers find me wet and ready, his satisfied smile makes me want to slap him or beg for more.

"Fuck you," I hiss, even as my body arches into his touch.

"That's the plan, baby." He unfastens his pants with one hand. "Right here, against this wall."

He thrusts inside me without warning, the brutal invasion making me cry out. My back scrapes against the wall with each powerful stroke, pain and pleasure blurring until I can't distinguish between them anymore.

"This is what you came for," Hunter growls against my ear, his breath hot and ragged. "Not to end things. To get fucked like the little slut you are."

I want to deny it, to preserve some shred of dignity, but my body betrays me as I clench around him. "Fuck you," I gasp instead, digging my nails deeper into his shoulders.

"You already are." He laughs darkly, then slaps my ass hard enough to make me yelp. "And loving every second."

His hand tangles in my hair, yanking my head back to expose my throat. His teeth find the sensitive spot where my neck meets my shoulder, biting down hard enough that I know it will bruise.

"Everyone will see my mark on you," he says, licking the spot he just bit. "They'll know you belong to me."

"I don't belong to anyone," I spit, even as my body contradicts me, my hips grinding desperately against his.

Hunter's laugh is cruel. "Your sister's fiancé is fucking

you against a wall, and you're coming on my cock like you'd die without it. I think we both know exactly who you belong to."

The mention of Olivia should douse my arousal like ice water. Instead, the forbidden nature of what we're doing sends another surge of heat through me. I'm sick, twisted for wanting this so badly.

"Hate yourself later," Hunter commands, reading my thoughts. "Right now, you're mine."

His fingers find my clit, circling roughly as his pace becomes punishing. I'm being used, claimed, marked, and God help me, I love it.

"Say it," he demands, his voice dangerous as he slows his movements, denying me the friction I crave. "Say you're mine."

"Please," I beg, shameless in my need.

"Say. You're. Mine." Each word is punctuated with a shallow thrust that leaves me whimpering.

"I'm yours," I confess, the admission tearing from somewhere deep inside me. "I'm yours, Hunter. Please—"

His fingers work me mercilessly, his rhythm perfectly matched to his thrusts, and something inside me shatters. The orgasm hits with shocking intensity, my entire body convulsing as waves of pleasure rip through me. I cry out, unable to hold back as my body releases in a way I've never experienced before, wetness gushing around his cock.

"Fuck," Hunter growls, looking down between us with savage satisfaction. "Look at you, soaking me."

I slump against him, trembling and disoriented, my body still pulsing with aftershocks. He holds me steady, his cock still rock-hard inside me.

"Why didn't you—" I begin, realizing he hasn't finished.

Hunter's laugh is dark against my ear before I can finish my sentence. "Oh baby, I'm not filling you until I've fucked you on every surface of this apartment." His teeth graze my earlobe. "That was just the appetizer."

Before I can process his words, he carries me away from the wall while I'm still impaled on him. My legs shake as he walks us into the living area, the movement of his cock inside me sending sparks of overstimulated pleasure through my sensitized body.

He sits on a sleek black leather couch, his hands gripping my hips. "Ride me," he commands, his voice leaving no room for refusal. "Show me how badly you want this."

Despite having just come harder than I ever have in my life, a desperate need claws through me again. I roll my hips experimentally, drawing a groan from him that sends a thrill through my body.

"That's it," he encourages, his hands guiding my movements. "Take what you want."

I lift myself, then sink back down on his length, my body welcoming him with embarrassing eagerness. He fills me, hitting places inside me that make my vision blur.

I grind against him in a languid rhythm, still sensitive from the first orgasm. Hunter grows impatient with my pace, his fingers digging painfully into my hips.

"Take off your dress," he commands.

I pull the fabric over my head, exposing my black lace bra. Hunter's eyes darken as he stares at my breasts, his expression almost feral. Without warning, he tears the delicate material, exposing me completely.

"Fuck," he growls, "your tits are perfect."

His mouth closes around one nipple, teeth grazing the sensitive peak before he bites down—hard enough to make me cry out, but not enough to hurt truly. The pain blurs into pleasure as his tongue soothes the sting.

"You like that?" His voice is dangerous, knowing. "When I mark what's mine?"

He moves to my other breast, treating it to the same rough attention. His teeth sink in deeper this time, leaving an impression of his dental pattern on my flesh. I arch into the sensation, a moan escaping my lips.

"Bounce on my cock like the greedy little whore you are," he demands, his hands guiding my hips into a faster rhythm. "Show me how badly you need it."

I comply, lifting myself and dropping back down, taking him deeper with each roll of my hips. The friction is exquisite, overwhelming.

"That's it," he hisses, his breath hot against my abused nipple. "Fuck yourself on me like you've been dreaming about since you first saw me."

His words send a fresh wave of heat through me. He's right because I have been dreaming of this.

"You're not your sister's perfect little Aurora anymore," he taunts, biting the underside of my breast hard enough to bruise. "You're mine now. My cock-hungry slut."

The combination of his cruel words, sharp teeth, and the perfect angle of his thrusts pushes me toward the edge again.

"Don't you dare fucking stop," he growls, sensing my impending orgasm. "Bounce until you come all over my cock."

I lose myself in his command, bouncing faster on his cock, chasing the pleasure building inside me. The degradation in his words shouldn't excite me. They should make me angry, make me stop, but instead, they fuel something dark and hungry inside me.

"That's right," Hunter growls, one hand tightening in my hair while the other grips my hip hard enough to bruise. "Show me what a filthy slut you are for me."

"Yes," I gasp, the admission burning my throat on its way out. "Yes, I'm yours."

His eyes flash with satisfaction. "Look at you, fucking yourself on your sister's fiancé." His teeth graze my neck. "So desperate for my cock you can't even think straight."

I should feel ashamed, but his words only drive me higher. Each degrading comment peels away another layer of restraint until I'm nothing but raw, exposed need.

"But you take me so perfectly," he adds, his voice softening momentarily. "Like you were made for my cock."

The praise mixed with degradation sends sparks down my spine. I grind harder, chasing the building pressure.

"Please," I beg, not even sure what I'm asking for.

"Please what?" Hunter's hand cracks across my ass, the sting making me clench around him. "Say it."

"Please let me come," I whimper, beyond pride now. "I need to come on your cock."

His laugh is dark as he pinches my nipple brutally. "Then come for me. Show me how good I make you feel."

The command breaks something inside me. I cry out as the orgasm rips through me, his name tearing from my throat repeatedly. "Hunter! Oh god, Hunter!"

I feel him grinding his teeth against my shoulder, fighting his own release, but my body's contractions are too much. He groans savagely as he bucks up, his cock pulsing inside me.

"Fuck," he snarls. "Your pussy gets so tight when you come. I can't—" His words dissolve into a primal growl as he empties himself inside me, his fingers digging into my flesh.

Before I can catch my breath, Hunter suddenly flips me over. I'm face-down on the leather couch, his body covering mine from behind. He's still inside me, impossibly hard despite his release moments ago.

"Don't think that because I've come this ends," he growls against my ear, rolling his hips in a slow, deliberate thrust that makes me gasp. The leather sticks to my sweat-slicked skin as he presses deeper.

His hand tangles in my hair, yanking my head back until my spine arches painfully. "I'm going to fuck you on every damn surface of this apartment." His teeth scrape along my shoulder, biting hard enough to make me whimper. "The kitchen counter, the shower, against every window. I want you to see yourself reflected in the glass while I take you from behind."

I can only moan in response, my body already responding to his renewed rhythm, impossibly sensitive yet craving more.

"By the time I'm done with you," he continues, his breath hot against my neck, "you'll be so full of my cum it will be spilling out of you for days." His free hand slides beneath me to circle my clit. "Every time you feel it dripping down your thighs, you'll remember who you belong to."

I should be horrified by his words, by how much they turn me on. This isn't me. I'm the good sister, the responsible one. Yet here I am, face pressed into expensive leather, my body responding eagerly to the man my sister is supposed to marry.

I've spent my entire life being the perfect stepdaughter, the supportive stepsister, building walls around myself after watching my father jump from that cliff. I've been so careful, so controlled.

But with Hunter, those walls crumble to dust. He sees the darkness inside me, the parts I've hidden from everyone else, including myself. And instead of being repulsed, he craves it. Demands it.

God help me, but I want to give him everything he asks for. I want to be consumed by him, even if it destroys me in the process.

22

HUNTER

I scan the updated operation reports projected on the wall, nodding at the quarterly numbers. The underground conference room at Vipers headquarters hums with quiet power as my colleagues review their sectors. Penn's narcotics division is up eighteen percent. Ari's blackmail portfolio has yielded three new judges under our control.

But throughout the presentation, I feel Jax's eyes on me. His attention shifts between the projection and my face, measuring my reactions with unusual intensity.

"The recruits are performing adequately," Blaine says, scrolling through the performance metrics. "Hansen exceeded expectations in his first asset acquisition."

I offer perfunctory comments on the financial structures we're using to launder the proceeds, but my focus splits between the data and Jax's persistent scrutiny. His fingers tap against the polished table. Three slow taps, pause, repeat. A pattern I recognize from when he's planning something.

"That covers the quarterly review," Grayson concludes,

shutting down the projection. "Unless there are strategic adjustments?"

"We're good," Jax says, standing first—a clear signal the meeting has ended. "Gentlemen, see your action items through by Friday."

The others file out, but when I move to follow, Jax's hand lands casually on my shoulder. "Hunter. A word."

We wait until the room empties, the reinforced door sealing with a pneumatic hiss. Jax leans against the edge of the table, studying me with that unreadable expression that's made many men crack under its weight.

"I see you've ignored our previous conversation about the Harrison situation," he says, voice deceptively conversational.

I maintain my neutral expression. "The merger is proceeding as planned."

His mouth quirks slightly. "Yet despite my explicit warning, Aurora Harrison was seen entering your building last night. Around ten thirty."

The casualness of his tone belies the message—this is no longer a first offense but a deliberate defiance of his earlier directive. He's still watching, and his patience is wearing thin.

I keep my face carefully neutral, though my pulse quickens. Jax doesn't repeat himself without consequences.

"As I explained before, Aurora is interested in the Harrison Foundation. These meetings ensure her cooperation for when I take over their business interests."

Jax's smile doesn't reach his eyes. "We've already discussed this 'approach.' My position hasn't changed—fucking the sister of your fiancée continues to complicate business arrangements. What has changed is my tolerance for your disregard of my concerns."

I maintain eye contact, though every instinct screams danger. Jax has become increasingly unpredictable these past months. Where he once ruled with cold logic, his decisions lately have felt arbitrary, driven by suspicion rather than strategy.

"The situation is under control," I say, voice level.

"Dominic thought the same before his 'reassignment,'" Jax says, the reference to our former weapons supplier hanging between us. Nobody's heard from Dominic since he questioned Jax's authority last month. "I don't typically need to repeat myself, Hunter. Consider this final courtesy a mark of our history together."

"Dominic was careless. I'm not."

Jax circles the table, each footstep deliberate. "Three members questioned my judgment this quarter. All three have been reassigned to more suitable positions."

Translation: they're either dead or wishing they were.

Marcus had suggested an alternative approach to the Davidson deal. Elena had data showing Jax's strategy for the eastern territory might be flawed. Both were gone within a week.

"Your judgment has built this organization," I say carefully. "Nobody questions that."

"Yet I sense hesitation from you, Hunter." He stops directly behind me. I resist the urge to turn. Showing weakness to Jax is never wise. "You've always been ambitious. Perhaps even... impatient."

The threat hangs between us. Jax doesn't tolerate perceived challenges to his authority, and lately, his threshold for what constitutes a challenge has narrowed dangerously.

"My ambition serves the Vipers," I respond. "Always has."

"See that it remains that way." His hand lands on my shoulder, fingers pressing slightly harder than necessary. "Your Harrison obsession. Ensure it doesn't become a problem."

I wait ten minutes after Jax leaves before texting Penn to meet at our secure location—an unmarked office three floors below my penthouse, swept weekly for surveillance. When he arrives, he's already holding a tumbler of bourbon, extending a second glass toward me.

"You look like you need this more than I do," Penn says, dropping into the leather chair across from me.

I take the drink but don't sip. "Jax knows about Aurora."

Penn nods, unsurprised. "That's not all he knows. He's had her under surveillance for the past week. Full package. Physical tail, telecommunications, the works."

My glass cracks slightly in my grip. "How did you find out?"

"Grayson mentioned Jax pulled three of his street team for a 'special assignment.' I traced the allocation code and it's the same one used for high-value targets." Penn leans forward. "Hunter, you need to be careful. Jax doesn't just see this as you breaking protocol. He sees your obvious emotional attachment as a weakness to exploit."

"You're certain about the surveillance?"

Penn pulls out his phone, shows me a requisition form with Aurora's name coded at the bottom. "Remember what happened with Marcus Chen?"

My jaw tightens. Marcus had been Jax's right hand for years—until he fell for a federal prosecutor's daughter. Three months later, Marcus was gone, his position filled without comment.

"Jax had Marcus eliminated for the same kind of distraction," Penn continues. "Called it a security risk. But we all knew it was because Marcus started prioritizing her over the Vipers."

I drain my glass, mind racing. "I need to move up my timeline."

"Or put it on hold," Penn suggests. "At least until Jax's paranoia finds a new target."

"That's not an option."

Penn studies me, a rare seriousness replacing his usual irreverence. "Then you'd better be prepared for what comes next. Because Jax won't just threaten you—he'll go after her first."

I slam my empty glass on the desk, rage building under my skin. "If Jax thinks he can dictate my personal life—"

"Hunter." Penn's voice cuts through my fury. "This isn't some business rival. It's Jax. The man who had his own cousin disappear for questioning his strategy in the city."

My phone buzzes. I ignore it.

"I'm aware of what Jax is capable of." I pace the room. "Which is why I need to accelerate everything. Get the Harrison merger done, and then end the engagement with Olivia, before dating Aurora."

"You're not thinking clearly." Penn rarely looks serious, but the concern in his eyes is genuine. "Jax doesn't issue warnings. When he sees a problem, he eliminates it."

My phone buzzes again. Then a third time in rapid succession.

"You should look at that," Penn says, nodding toward my phone. "Could be important."

I grab my phone, expecting another message from Aurora. Instead, I see three notifications from an encrypted number. Jax's private channel.

The first message contains an image. I open it to find a high-resolution photo of Aurora at her desk at Bloom's

Press, taken from an angle that could only come from the building directly across from her office.

The second shows her leaving the building, unaware of the camera tracking her movements.

The third message contains no image, just five words:

"Your distraction is a concern."

I stare at the messages, my fingers tightening around the phone until I hear the faint creak of metal and glass. My pulse hammers in my temples as rage builds like a physical force inside me.

"What is it?" Penn asks, leaning forward.

Without a word, I turn the screen toward him. His usual irreverence vanishes as he studies the photos.

"Fuck," he breathes. "He's not being subtle."

"He's threatening her." My voice sounds foreign to my own ears. "This crosses a line."

Penn sets his glass down carefully. "Hunter, think this through. Jax doesn't make empty threats. If you push back—"

"If I do nothing, he'll see it as weakness." I glare at Penn. "Jax respects power and decisiveness. Backing down now will only confirm his suspicions."

"Or buy you time to maneuver," Penn counters.

I shake my head. "Time isn't the issue. Perception is." I stop at the window, looking out at the city below. Our city, our territory. "Jax is testing boundaries. Mine specifically."

My phone buzzes again. Another message from Jax:

"Meeting. My office. One hour."

Penn reads it over my shoulder and winces. "He's escalating. Fast."

"Good." I slide the phone into my pocket. "Let him."

"That's suicide. He's clearly making a move against you."

I turn to face Penn, decision made. "Then I'll have to make mine first."

I press the secure call button on my watch. Seconds later, Grayson's voice comes through.

"What's the situation?" he asks without preamble.

"Jax is making his play. Implement contingency protocol Delta."

There's a moment of silence before Grayson responds. "Understood. Timeline?"

"Immediate. I need everything in place within the hour."

"Consider it done."

The line goes dead. Penn stares at me, expression unreadable.

"You've been planning for this," he says. Not a question.

"I've planned for every possibility since the day I joined the Vipers."

"And Aurora?"

I check my watch. Fifty-three minutes until I meet with Jax.

"Secure her. Now."

23

AURORA

Something's off. I can't quite place it, but the sensation of being watched prickles along my spine as I walk from the parking garage to my office building. I glance over my shoulder. I don't see anything unusual, just the typical morning crowd hurrying to work.

You're being paranoid, Aurora.

I shake it off and push through the revolving doors into the Bloom's Press lobby. After yesterday's chaos with Olivia's surprise London trip and my... encounter with Hunter, my nerves are frayed. That's all this is.

By mid-morning, the feeling returns. While reviewing layout proofs at my desk, I catch a glimpse of movement outside my window. A man in a dark jacket quickly turns away when I look up. My heart stutters, but I rationalize it. Hundreds of people work in the building across the street.

When lunchtime arrives, I head to the little café two blocks down. As I wait for my order, I notice the same man from earlier, sitting alone at a corner table, pretending to read something on his phone. But the angle is all wrong, and his eyes keep darting toward me.

Ice floods my veins. This isn't a coincidence.

I grab my lunch to go and hurry back to the office, taking a deliberately circuitous route. When I spot him again, half a block behind me, matching my pace, my suspicions crystallize into certainty.

Someone is following me.

Back at my desk, I try to focus on work, but my hands shake as I type. At five o'clock, I gather my things and take the elevator down. Through the glass doors, I can see him. The same dark jacket guy, wearing sunglasses despite the cloudy day and positioned casually against a newspaper stand.

Waiting for me.

With my purse clutched against my chest, I retreat to the lobby restroom and lock myself in a stall. With trembling fingers, I pull out my phone and call the one person I know can help.

Hunter answers on the first ring. "Aurora."

"Someone's following me," I whisper, voice cracking. "All day. The same man. He's outside the building now."

"Stay inside. Don't move." His voice is deadly calm. "I'm three minutes away."

When I peek out the lobby doors exactly four minutes later, I see Hunter's Bentley screech to a halt at the curb. He emerges, scanning the street with glacial focus. When his eyes lock on the man in the dark jacket, his expression transforms into a terrifying fury carved into every line of his face.

Hunter strides toward me, wrapping a protective arm around my shoulders. The man in the dark jacket melts into the crowd before Hunter can reach him.

"You were right," Hunter says, his voice tight as he scans the street. "That man was watching you."

"Who is he? What does he want?" My voice trembles.

Hunter guides me toward his car, opening the passenger door. "Get in."

Once we're both inside the Bentley, Hunter turns to me, his expression grave. "It's not uncommon in my position to attract unwanted attention. Someone's been tracking my movements, and now they're watching you too."

"But why me?"

"Because they've seen us together." His fingers grip the steering wheel until his knuckles turn white. "Business rivals. They're looking for leverage against me."

Something in his explanation doesn't quite fit, but fear clouds my judgment. "What do we do?"

"First, I'm taking you home. I need to check your apartment."

During the drive, Hunter keeps glancing in the rearview mirror. The casual possessiveness I'd found both terrifying and thrilling before now feels like a shield.

At my apartment, Hunter doesn't wait for an invitation. He follows me inside, immediately walking through each room.

"What exactly are you looking for?" I ask as he examines my light fixtures.

"Security vulnerabilities." He runs his fingers along my windowsills, behind picture frames, under the coffee table. "If they're watching you outside, they might have tried to access your apartment."

I watch as he checks the electrical outlets, unplugs my clock radio, examines it, then plugs it back in. He moves to the smoke detector, standing on a chair to inspect it closely.

"Is that necessary for a security check?" I ask.

Hunter removes something tiny from behind the detector. "Yes. Because this isn't a security feature." He holds up what looks like a black grain of rice between his fingers. "It's a listening device."

My blood runs cold. "Someone's been... hearing everything?"

Hunter crushes it between his fingers. "Not anymore."

I stare at the crushed remains of the listening device in Hunter's palm, cold fear spreading through my chest.

"Who is doing this, Hunter?" I ask again, more forcefully this time. "And don't just say 'business rivals.' I need a real answer."

Hunter's expression shifts subtly—a tightening around his eyes, a slight clench of his jaw. He tosses the broken device into my trash can and wipes his hands.

"It's likely someone working for Westcott Technologies," he says smoothly. "They've been trying to sabotage my latest acquisition. Standard corporate espionage."

I watch him as he speaks. Something doesn't add up. His explanation is too rehearsed, too clean. And if this were just about business, why would they be following me specifically?

"So why not just bug your office? Why follow me?" I press.

Hunter runs a hand through his hair. His usual composed demeanor shows the faintest crack.

"They're trying to find my vulnerabilities." His eyes meet mine with an intensity that would normally distract me. "You're becoming one of them."

The words sound sincere, but there's something hollow behind them, like they're only part of a larger truth he's deliberately withholding.

"Hunter, I need to know what I'm dealing with." I step closer. "If someone's listening to my conversations and following me, I deserve to know exactly why."

His phone vibrates. He checks it, and I catch a glimpse of the text before he turns it away:

SECURE HER NOW. JAX INBOUND.

"Who's Jax?" I ask.

Hunter's expression hardens instantly. The room temperature seems to have dropped by 10 degrees.

"No one you need to worry about." His voice is cold steel, nothing like the silky persuasion he typically uses with me. "Pack a bag. You're staying with me tonight."

"I'm not going anywhere until you tell me what's really happening."

Hunter's eyes narrow. I can practically see him weighing how much to reveal against how much he needs my compliance.

"I asked you a question." My voice comes out steadier than I feel. "Who is Jax?"

Hunter's expression is completely void of the humanity I've come to associate with him. This is a different Hunter; one I don't recognize.

"This isn't a negotiation, Aurora." He steps closer, towering over me. "You're in danger. We need to leave. Now."

"Not until you tell me what's happening." I cross my arms, planting my feet firmly despite the fear tightening my chest. "I deserve to know why I'm being followed, why my apartment is bugged, and who this Jax person is."

Hunter checks his watch, jaw clenched. "We don't have time for this."

"Make time."

He stares at me for a long moment, then exhales sharply. "Jax is... a business associate. Someone I work with closely."

"And why is he 'inbound'? Why does he want you to 'secure' me?" I press.

"Because he's concerned about our relationship." Hunter's voice drops, becomes more controlled. "As I said, you're becoming a vulnerability."

"That doesn't explain the surveillance."

Hunter runs a hand through his hair again. "Jax runs a security team for our organization. The surveillance was likely his order, not a competitor's."

The pieces suddenly click together. "Wait. Your own people are following me? Your business associate ordered someone to bug my apartment?"

Hunter's phone buzzes again. His eyes dart to it, then back to me with new urgency.

"Aurora, please. Pack what you need. I'll explain everything once you're safe."

"Safe from what? From your own associate?"

The look that crosses Hunter's face tells me more than his words do. There's real fear there, not for himself, but for me.

The urgency in Hunter's eyes finally breaks through my stubbornness. Whatever's happening, his fear for me is genuine.

"Fine," I say, heading to my bedroom. "But you're explaining everything once we're in the car."

I grab my overnight bag from the closet and start throwing in essentials. My underwear, toiletries, and a change of clothes. Hunter follows me, leaning against the doorframe with his arms crossed.

"Pack enough for a few days," he says.

I shoot him a glare. "A few days? I have work tomorrow."

"Call in sick."

"You can't just upend my entire life because your 'associate' is having surveillance issues," I snap, cramming a sweater into my bag with more force than necessary.

"I'm trying to protect you."

"From a problem you created." I grab my phone charger, yanking it from the wall. "If you hadn't started whatever this is with me, I wouldn't need protection."

Hunter moves toward me, and despite my anger, my body responds to his proximity. "Are you saying you regret what's happened between us?"

"I'm saying I regret the mysterious threats part." I zip my bag closed with a sharp tug. "The sex was fine."

His eyebrow arches. "Fine?"

"Don't fish for compliments when I'm being forced into witness protection because of your sketchy business partners."

A hint of a smile tugs at his lips. "It's not witness protection."

"Whatever this is." I grab my purse, checking for my wallet and keys. "And just so we're clear, I'm pissed about this. About all of it."

Hunter takes my bag, his fingers brushing mine. "I like you pissed. It's sexy."

"Save the charm for someone who your colleagues aren't stalking."

As we head for the door, I pause to grab my favorite book from the nightstand. Hunter watches me curiously.

"Never know when you'll be stuck in a billionaire's panic room," I mutter, shoving it into my purse.

He places his hand at the small of my back, guiding me toward the door. "It's a penthouse, not a panic room."

"Is there a difference when you're essentially a prisoner?"

We step into the hallway, and Hunter checks in both directions before motioning me forward. His hand presses against the small of my back, protective rather than possessive. The warmth of his palm seeps through my blouse, a reminder of how easily my body responds to his touch.

In the elevator, I face him directly. "I want the truth, Hunter. No more vague explanations or half-answers. Who exactly is Jax, and why is he watching me?"

Hunter's gaze holds mine, something shifting in his expression. For a moment, the mask slips.

"Jax King is the leader of an organization I belong to. We're... associates, but that term doesn't capture the full scope." He exhales slowly. "Our relationship operates on absolute loyalty and discretion. When he learned about you, about us, he viewed it as a liability."

"What kind of organization requires that level of control?"

The elevator doors open to the parking garage. Hunter guides me toward his car, scanning our surroundings.

"The kind that doesn't allow distractions or divided loyalties," he says, opening the passenger door for me. "The kind where weakness gets exploited."

Once we're both inside, I turn to him. "And I'm your weakness."

His hands grip the steering wheel, knuckles white. "You're becoming something I didn't anticipate."

"Which is?"

He stares straight ahead. "Something I'm not willing to sacrifice."

The raw honesty in his voice catches me off guard. For the first time since I've known him, Hunter sounds vulnerable.

"I won't let anything happen to you," he says, his voice low and fierce. "Even if it means going against Jax."

My heart stutters in my chest. This dangerous, complex man is willing to risk everything to keep me safe. And despite all the reasons I should run in the opposite direction, despite knowing so little about who he really is beneath the wealth and power and control, I'm falling for him.

The realization terrifies me. Because the truth is, I don't really know Hunter Reed at all. I only know the parts he's chosen to reveal, fragments of a man whose full picture might horrify me. And still, my heart races when he looks at me like I'm the only thing that matters.

God help me, what am I getting myself into?

24

HUNTER

I drive along the coastal road with Aurora beside me, silence stretching between us. The city lights fade behind as we climb higher into the cliffs. My knuckles whiten against the steering wheel. Taking her to the penthouse isn't enough, not with Jax's resources. We need distance, isolation, and time.

"This isn't the way to your penthouse," Aurora says, tension sharpening her voice.

"We're going to my cliff house."

Her head snaps toward me. "We're what?"

"The property next door to your father's. More secure. Harder to access."

Aurora scowls but doesn't say another word. The tension in the car is palpable.

I pull through the gates, the security system recognizing my vehicle. The house emerges from the darkness, glass and stone perched on the edge of existence. Unlike the Harrison mansion with its old-world grandeur, mine is all sharp angles and modern defiance against the cliffside.

Inside, Aurora moves straight to the wall of windows overlooking the churning ocean. The moonlight catches her profile, illuminating the determined set of her jaw. She's never looked more beautiful, or more dangerous to everything I've built.

"I need answers, Hunter. Real ones." She turns. "Who exactly is Jax King? What organization are you part of? Why does he consider me a threat?"

The questions hang between us like smoke. I could lie, since I've become an expert at half-truths and omissions, but part of me wants her to know. Wants someone to see the darkness I've cultivated.

But revealing everything would mean losing her. And despite every instinct honed over years of control, I can't bear that thought.

I cross the room, drawn to her like gravity. "Aurora—"

"Don't." She raises a hand. "Don't distract me with... whatever this is between us. I deserve the truth."

She's right. She deserves answers, safety, and someone far better than me.

Instead, I take her face in my hands and kiss her.

It's not calculated. Not strategic. For perhaps the first time in my adult life, I act purely on need. Her lips part in surprise beneath mine, and I deepen the kiss, backing her against the window. My hands slide into her hair, cradling her head as though she might shatter in my grasp.

I need her more than my next breath. More than the control that has defined my existence.

My kiss becomes savage, demanding. Something inside snaps. The thin veneer of restraint I've been clinging to. I pull back, her lips swollen from my assault, her eyes wide with anticipation and a hunger that matches my own.

"On the sofa. Now." My voice drops to a dangerous growl as I walk her backward.

Her breathing quickens, chest rising and falling rapidly. "Hunter—"

"Questions later." I guide her roughly toward the low-slung leather sofa dominating the center of the room. "I need to taste you first."

The moonlight spills across her face, highlighting the flush spreading across her cheeks. I push her down onto the sofa, dropping to my knees between her legs. My hands slide up her thighs, pushing her skirt higher until it bunches around her waist.

"Lie back," I command, hooking my fingers into the thin fabric of her underwear. "Let me devour you."

She hesitates only a moment before complying, her head falling back against the cushions as I tear the delicate material away. The sound of ripping fabric echoes through the room.

"These are in my way," I mutter, tossing the ruined underwear aside.

I grip her thighs, spreading them wide, exposing her completely to my gaze. Mine. The thought burns through me like wildfire as I lower my head. The first broad stroke of my tongue makes her gasp, back arching off the sofa.

"Stay still," I growl against her sensitive flesh. "You'll take what I give you."

My mouth returns to her heat, tongue circling her clit before dipping lower. I feast on her like a starving man, hands gripping her thighs tight enough to bruise. Her taste is addictively sweet and uniquely hers. I devour her relentlessly, my tongue exploring every fold, every sensitive spot that makes her moan.

When her hands tangle in my hair, I growl and redouble my efforts, sucking her clit between my lips as my fingers dig into her flesh. Her hips buck, pushing her pussy harder against my mouth.

The taste of her drives me wild, her surrender fueling an insatiable need I can't control. Her moans fill the room as my tongue works relentlessly. The evidence of her desire coats my lips, my chin. She's marking me as thoroughly as I've marked her.

It's not enough.

I pull back abruptly, breathing hard. Aurora whimpers at the loss, her eyes heavy-lidded with desire.

"Stand up," I order, my voice rough with need.

She blinks, disoriented. I've never seen anything more beautiful than Aurora Harrison flushed and desperate from my touch.

"Now, Aurora." My hands move to my belt, unfastening it with practiced efficiency.

She rises on shaky legs, watching as I strip away my pants and boxers in one fluid motion. My cock springs free, hard and aching for her.

I lie back on the sofa, resting against the leather cushions. "I want your pussy on my face while you suck my cock."

Her eyes widen, desire darkening them to midnight blue. "Hunter—"

"Don't make me wait." The command in my voice brooks no argument.

Aurora moves toward me; her skirt is still bunched around her waist. I grab her hips, positioning her above me.

"Sixty-nine," I instruct. "Your mouth on my cock while I finish what I started."

She straddles my face with trembling thighs, lowering herself until I can resume my feast. My tongue plunges inside her as her lips tentatively wrap around my cockhead.

I grip her ass, pulling her more firmly against my mouth, encouraging her to grind against my face. My groan vibrates against her sensitive flesh when she takes me deeper.

"That's it," I growl against her slick heat. "Take all of me."

Aurora moans around my cock, the vibration sending pleasure coursing through me. She's lost to sensation now, her body responding to my every command as she rocks against my mouth while working her lips up and down my length.

Her mouth works my cock with growing confidence, taking me deeper with each downward motion. I grip her ass harder, burying my face between her thighs as her wetness coats my chin. The dual sensation of her hot mouth sliding down my shaft while my tongue plunges inside her threatens to unravel my control.

"Fuck," I growl against her slick flesh when she hollows her cheeks, creating suction that nearly makes me lose my mind. Her moans vibrate around my cock as I devour her, my tongue circling her clit before diving back inside.

Heat builds at the base of my spine, pleasure coiling tight. I'm too close, too soon. With a growl, I grip her hips and lift her off my face.

"Stop," I command, voice hoarse with need. Her mouth releases me with a wet pop, her breathing ragged. "Turn around. I want to watch your face when I fill you."

Aurora's eyes are glazed with desire as she shifts, repositioning herself to straddle my hips. I grip my cock, holding it steady as she hovers above me.

"Take what's yours," I demand. The sight of her all flushed and desperate makes me harder than I've ever been. "Show me how badly you need it."

She sinks slowly, her body stretching to accommodate me. I hiss through clenched teeth as her tight heat engulfs me, inch by agonizing inch.

"That's it," I growl, hands gripping her hips hard enough to bruise. "Your sister's fiancé, buried deep inside you. How does it feel to be so fucking filthy?"

Her walls clench around me at the forbidden words. I thrust upward, driving deeper.

"This pussy belongs to me now," I growl, guiding her movements. "Say it. Tell me who owns this perfect cunt."

"You do," she gasps, beginning to ride me with abandon. "Only you, Hunter."

"That's right." I reach up to grip her throat, applying just enough pressure to make her eyes widen. "Every inch of you is mine to use, to mark, to ruin for anyone else."

Aurora rides me with wild abandon, her body claiming mine as thoroughly as I'm claiming hers. Her head falls back, dark hair cascading down her spine as she moves. The moonlight streaming through the windows paints her skin silver, turning her into something ethereal I never deserved, but I'd destroy anyone to keep.

"Look at me," I demand, tightening my grip on her throat just enough to guide her gaze back to mine. "I want to see your face when you come apart for me."

Her eyes lock with mine, pupils wide with desire. The way her vulnerability is unfiltered hits me hard. No one has ever looked at me like this. Like they see the monster beneath the mask and want me anyway.

I thrust up harder, meeting her movements with punishing force. The sound of skin slapping against skin fills the room, punctuated by her desperate moans and my grunts. I release her throat to grip her ass with both hands, controlling her pace.

"Whose cock is stretching this perfect pussy?" I growl, driving deeper.

"Yours," she gasps, her inner walls clenching around me. "I only ever want yours, Hunter."

I've built empires, destroyed lives, held the fate of powerful men in my hands, but nothing compares to hearing Aurora Harrison surrender to me.

I feel her body tightening, trembling on the edge of release. My thumb finds her clit, circling the sensitive bud as she continues to ride me.

"Come for me," I command. "Show me how much you need me."

Her rhythm falters as pleasure overtakes her. Her inner walls pulse around my cock as she cries out, nails digging crescents into my chest. The sight of her completely undone by my touch pushes me dangerously close to the edge.

I grip her hips harder, holding her in place as I continue thrusting up into her oversensitive body.

With one powerful thrust, I flip her beneath me, pinning her to the sofa. Her hair fans across the leather cushions, eyes wide with surprise and desire.

"I need to be deeper," I growl, hooking one of her legs over my shoulder. "I need to fill you."

I drive into her with savage intensity, each thrust claiming her more thoroughly than the last. Her walls clench around me, drawing me deeper into her heat.

"You're mine," I snarl, picking up pace. My hips slam against hers, the sound of flesh meeting flesh echoing through the room. "Say it."

"Yours," she gasps, her nails digging into my shoulders. "Only yours, Hunter."

The pressure builds at the base of my spine, my rhythm

becoming erratic as I chase release. Aurora's eyes lock with mine, pupils blown wide with pleasure and a deeper emotion that threatens to break through walls I've built over a lifetime.

"I'm going to fill you," I rasp, feeling my control slipping. "Mark you from the inside out."

Her inner walls flutter around me, her third orgasm building. The knowledge that I can reduce this fierce, independent woman to trembling need beneath me is intoxicating.

With a primal growl, I bury myself to the hilt and explode inside her, pumping her full of my release. Wave after wave of pleasure tears through me as I empty myself. My orgasm triggers her own as she squirts all over my cock, moaning loudly as her cunt squeezes me like a vise.

"Fuck," I groan, continuing to thrust through mine and her orgasm. "Take every drop."

I collapse against her, still buried inside, unwilling to break our connection. My breath comes in ragged pants against her neck as I grasp her face between my hands.

"An eternity," I murmur against her lips, "fucking and breeding you will never be enough."

The honesty in my voice surprises even me. Hunter Reed. A man who professes to care about no one is falling in love with a woman. Aurora Harrison. His fiancée's sister.

25

AURORA

I wake to warmth and the steady rise and fall of Hunter's chest against my back. His arms are wrapped around me possessively; one hand splayed across my stomach. For a moment, I breathe, allowing myself to enjoy the sensation of being completely enveloped by him.

When I shift slightly, I realize he's already awake. I turn in his arms to face him, finding his intense gray-blue eyes studying me.

My chest tightens painfully. This can't continue, not like this.

"You need to break it off with Olivia," I say, my voice quiet but firm. "And I'll tell her the truth about us."

Hunter's thumb strokes my cheek, his eyes never leaving mine. "I was planning to end it as soon as she returns from London."

"I need to be honest with her," I continue, guilt twisting inside me. "She's my sister. I've already betrayed her enough by being with you behind her back."

He nods, surprising me with his immediate agreement. "We'll handle it however you want."

I take a deep breath, thinking about my conversation with Olivia before she left. "She actually didn't seem that bothered about potentially calling off the wedding. I think your arrangement was more important to our father than to her."

Hunter's expression doesn't change. "That doesn't surprise me."

"But…" I hesitate, considering the implications. "Maybe we should frame it as her idea? Like, she decided to break it off with you. Olivia is obsessed with appearances, and this way she saves face in front of her friends and social media followers."

His jaw tightens. "As long as the result is the same, I don't care how it happens. I want you. Publicly. No more hiding."

I curl deeper into Hunter's embrace, savoring the weight of his arm around me. The past twenty-four hours have been a whirlwind, both terrifying and exhilarating all at once. Outside, waves crash against the cliffs, but in here, wrapped in Hunter's expensive sheets, I feel strangely safe despite everything.

"Are you hungry?" Hunter murmurs against my hair. "I can have something prepared."

I shake my head, not wanting to break this bubble we've created. "Not yet."

His fingers trace lazy patterns on my bare shoulder. Though we're hiding from this Jax person and whatever organization Hunter belongs to, I've never felt more at peace. It's strange how little I know about what's really happening, yet how completely I trust him.

"We should probably talk more about Jax," I say, though I make no move to pull away. "I still don't understand who he is or why he sees me as your weakness."

Hunter's body tenses slightly beneath mine. "Later. Right now, I want to be here with you."

I'm about to press further when my phone buzzes on the nightstand. Reluctantly, I reach for it.

The blissful warmth evaporates instantly when I see Olivia's name on the screen.

Surprise! I came home early. Where are you? Been trying to reach you all day. Getting worried.

My heart pounds as I sit up, clutching the sheet to my chest. "Olivia's back. She's at home right now."

Hunter sits up beside me, immediately alert. "You can't go back there."

"But if I don't, she'll really worry," I say, panic rising. "I can't exactly tell her I'm hiding out with her fiancé."

"If Jax has men watching your estate, you'll be walking right into danger."

I stare at my phone, Olivia's text glowing accusingly. The perfect bubble we'd been in just seconds ago has shattered completely. I have no explanation for where I've been, no way to return home safely, and no idea how to respond to my sister without lying even more.

Hunter's brow furrows in thought as he watches me stare at my phone. "Tell her you're at your father's estate. Say you needed space, time to think after your mother's anniversary."

I look up at him, my fingers still hovering over the keyboard. It's not a terrible idea. I have disappeared to the cliff house before when things got overwhelming.

"I don't know if that will work," I say, worrying my bottom lip between my teeth. "If I tell her I'm here, she might drive out to join me. Olivia hates being alone at the apartment."

Hunter's expression shifts. His hand slides up my bare back, warm and steady against my skin.

"Maybe that would be perfect," he says, his voice low. "If she comes out here, we could talk to her together. Put our plan to her about ending the engagement."

I pull away slightly, staring at him. "You want to tell her about us? Here? Now?"

"Think about it, Aurora." Hunter sits up fully, the sheet pooling around his waist. "It's neutral ground. If she reacts badly, she can have space immediately."

My heart races at the thought. I'd imagined having this conversation with Olivia alone first, softening the blow before introducing Hunter into the equation.

"Don't you think it would be better if I spoke to her one-on-one initially? This is going to be a shock no matter what, but both of us confronting her at once feels..."

"Honest," Hunter finishes for me. "Direct. No more secrets or manipulation."

I run a hand through my tangled hair. "She's going to hate me."

"She already told you she doesn't love me," Hunter reminds me. "That this was just business for her."

"There's a difference between not loving your fiancé and finding out he's sleeping with your sister," I counter.

I stare at my phone, heart hammering against my ribs as I type a response to Olivia.

I'm at Dad's cliff house. Needed some space after Mom's anniversary. Just taking some time to clear my head.

My thumb hovers over the send button for a few seconds before I finally press it. The message disappears with a swoosh, and I exhale shakily.

"Do you think she'll believe me?" I ask Hunter, who's

watching me intently from his position beside me on the bed.

"It's the truth, partially," he says. "The best lies always are."

I set my phone down on the nightstand, but keep glancing at it every few seconds. The three dots appear almost immediately, showing Olivia is typing a response. They disappear, then reappear again. My stomach twists with anxiety.

"She's typing something... deleting it... typing again," I narrate to Hunter, who places a reassuring hand on my thigh over the sheets.

Finally, my phone buzzes with her reply.

Poor thing! I'm coming out there right now. Don't want you to be alone with your thoughts. I'll bring wine and those pastries you like from Bellini's.

My pulse quickens. "She's coming here. Right now." I turn to Hunter, panic rising in my chest. "What do we do? What do I say to her?"

Hunter remains calm, his expression unreadable as he takes my phone and reads Olivia's message. "It's for the best. We need to deal with this situation head-on."

"But not like this," I protest, running my fingers nervously through my tangled hair. "Not with you here, where she'll immediately know we've been—"

My phone buzzes again, cutting me off. I snatch it from Hunter's hand and read the new message.

I can't come out after all. The weather forecast has just been updated. There's a massive storm heading toward the coast. They're saying it could be bad. Flash flood warnings and everything. Stay safe out there, okay? We'll catch up when you get back to the city. Love you! xo

Relief washes over me so intensely that I fall back against the pillows. "She's not coming. There's a storm."

Hunter studies my face. "Why do I sense you're relieved that she's not coming?"

I sit up, pulling the sheet with me as I create distance between us. "You don't understand."

"Then explain it to me." His voice is calm, but there's an edge to it that makes me shiver.

"I hate that I've betrayed her like this." The words tumble out, heavy with the guilt I've been carrying. "She's my sister, Hunter. My entire life, she's been the one person I could count on. After Mom died, after everything..." I shake my head, trying to organize my chaotic thoughts. "And now look at me. Sleeping with her fiancé, lying to her face. What kind of person does that make me?"

Hunter reaches for my hand, but I pull away.

"And the idea of telling her..." My voice cracks. "Sitting her down and watching her face when she realizes that while she was in London, we were..." I can't even finish the sentence.

"She has to know at some point, Aurora." Hunter's tone is matter-of-fact, as if we're discussing a business transaction rather than potentially shattering my relationship with my sister. "The longer this goes on, the worse it will be when she finds out."

"I know that," I snap, frustration bubbling up. "Don't you think I know that? But this isn't just about us getting what we want. There are consequences. Real, painful consequences that I'll have to live with long after the initial confession."

Hunter's jaw tightens. "And you think I won't?"

"It's different for you." I meet his gaze directly. "You've made it clear this engagement was nothing more than a business arrangement for you. But Olivia is my stepsister. My family. The only real family I have."

Hunter sighs heavily, reaching for his phone on the nightstand. The moment he reads the text, he swears under his breath, his body tensing beside me.

"What's wrong?" I ask, pulling the sheet higher around me.

He runs a hand through his disheveled hair, eyes fixed on the screen. "I forgot. Our annual masquerade is Saturday night."

"Saturday? That's in two days." I sit up straighter against the headboard. "Today's Thursday."

"I know." His jaw tightens as he types a response. "They want me back in town. Now. There's preparation that requires my presence."

A realization hits me. "Wait, the masquerade... Is that the one at the Reed Tower? The charity event?" I lean forward, my hair falling across my shoulders. "You invited Olivia and me to it. She's been talking about it ever since."

Hunter's head snaps up, his piercing eyes meeting mine. "You can't come."

"What do you mean I can't come? Olivia would absolutely kill me if I missed it." I shake my head, incredulous at his demand. "She's so excited about it."

"Aurora." The way he says my name is sharp, almost dangerous. "You're not understanding the situation. Your life might be in danger if you attend."

I stare at him, confusion and frustration building. "Why would my life be in danger at your ball? That doesn't make any sense."

Hunter's expression darkens as he seems to battle with himself. Finally, his shoulders drop slightly.

"Fine. If you insist on attending, you always stay near

me." His voice leaves no room for negotiation. "Not with your sister, not with your friends. With me. Do you understand?"

I shake my head emphatically. "How would that look? Me hanging around my sister's fiancé all night instead of being with her? Everyone would notice." The sheet pools around my waist as I sit up straighter. "Two of our friends already know some of what is going on between us."

Hunter's jaw clenches. A muscle ticks beneath his skin as he leans closer, his eyes never leaving mine. "Tell her."

"What?"

"Tell Olivia about us. Before the masquerade." His voice drops to that commanding tone that sends shivers down my spine. "End this charade now."

I press my palms against my eyes, trying to think clearly. "I can't just text her something like that. And I can't tell her on the phone either. This needs to be face-to-face."

"Then do it tomorrow." Hunter reaches for his phone, already making plans. "We need to plan to head back to town anyway. This storm could get dangerous."

"Tomorrow," I repeat, the word feeling heavy on my tongue. After tomorrow, everything will be different. My relationship with Olivia might be irreparably damaged.

Hunter's fingers move rapidly across his phone screen. "I'll have people watching the Harrison estate. Beyond your father's normal security."

"What? Why?"

"Because Jax knows about you." His eyes flick up to mine, deadly serious. "And until I handle this situation, you're vulnerable. Anyone close to you is vulnerable."

My stomach drops. "Olivia too?"

"I've already arranged protection for her, though she won't know it." He sets his phone down and takes my face between his hands. "I won't let anything happen to either of you."

His hands cradle my face, and before I can respond, Hunter's mouth claims mine in a desperate, possessive kiss. My body responds instantly despite all my racing thoughts and fears. His tongue slips between my parted lips, and I melt against him, fingers threading through his hair.

The sheet falls away as he pulls me onto his lap, his hands exploring my bare skin with a purpose that makes me forget everything but this moment. He tastes like coffee and something darker, something uniquely Hunter.

"Mine," he growls between kisses, one hand gripping my hip, the other sliding up my spine.

I arch against him, the power of his touch sending electric pulses through my body. But even as I surrender to the sensation, a voice in the back of my mind whispers a warning.

What am I doing? What have I gotten myself into?

This man is engaged to my sister. He's in some kind of dangerous organization with people who apparently want to hurt me. I know almost nothing about him except that he's capable of making me forget all my principles with just a touch.

His lips trail down my neck, and I gasp, momentarily losing my train of thought. I clutch his shoulders, my nails digging into his skin.

The storm outside intensifies, rain lashing against the windows as if nature itself is warning me. But I can't stop. Don't want to stop. Even as I wonder about the consequences—about Jax, about Olivia, about this masquerade he insists I can't attend—my body betrays me, seeking more of him.

"Hunter," I breathe, pulling back just enough to look

into his eyes. Those stormy blue-gray depths reveal nothing of the secrets he keeps, only hunger and something that looks dangerously close to possession.

26

HUNTER

Every detail matters. I scan the ballroom of the Reed Technologies headquarters, watching my security team position themselves at strategic points throughout the venue. Glass chandeliers catch the afternoon light, casting crystalline patterns across the marble floor where hundreds of the city's elite will gather tonight behind their masks and facades.

"The west entrance needs additional coverage." I point to the blueprint spread across the temporary command table. "Position Davis and Lowell here. I want eyes on every entrance and exit."

My head of security nods, making notes while I check my watch. Seven hours until the masquerade begins. Seven hours until I see Aurora again.

Aurora. Her name alone sends heat through my veins. The memory of her skin against mine at the cliff house, the way her breath caught when I touched her—

"Mr. Reed?" My security chief's voice pulls me back. "About the guest list verification protocol?"

I refocus. "Triple-check every ID against the biometric database. No exceptions."

Penn saunters in, surveying my elaborate security setup with an amused expression. He waits until my team disperses before approaching.

"Planning for a war rather than a ball?" He picks up one of the security badges and examines it. "Fifteen armed men, facial recognition at every entrance, and..." he gestures to the screens showing real-time surveillance feeds, "enough cameras to make the NSA jealous."

I don't take the bait. "Jax will be here tonight."

"He attends every year." Penn shrugs. "Why the paranoia now?"

"He's had Aurora under surveillance for over a week." My voice drops to ensure only Penn hears me. "Not just casual observation. This is full surveillance. Tracking devices on her car, bugs in her apartment, men following her movements."

Penn's playful demeanor vanishes. "Shit."

"Exactly." I tap a command into my tablet, bringing up a detailed layout of tonight's security positions. "I'm not taking chances. I've positioned our people at every critical point. Grayson's handling Jax's arrival personally."

"You think he'd try something here? At your public event?"

"I think Jax considers her my weakness." I meet Penn's eyes. "And he eliminates weaknesses."

Penn tosses the security badge onto the table and checks his watch. "As much as I'd love to stay and watch you micromanage your security team, we've got that leadership meeting at Vipers in thirty."

"Fuck." I'd lost track of time preparing for tonight's event. "Jax call it?"

"Three hours ago. Something about 'organizational realignment.'" Penn makes air quotes, his expression darkening. "And when Jax wants to realign things…"

"Someone gets broken." I grab my phone and send a final set of instructions to my head of security before nodding toward the exit. "Let's take my car."

Minutes later, we're sliding into the back seat of my Bentley. Hansen, my driver, closes the door behind us.

"The usual location, sir?" Hansen asks through the intercom.

"Yes. And take the tunnel route."

Penn sprawls across his half of the back seat, loosening his tie. "You know, most people just say, 'the office' instead of 'the usual location.' Theatrical bastard."

"Says the man who branded his initials on last month's trafficking scumbag we caught."

"That was different. Sent a message." Penn grins, unrepentant. "Besides, you've done worse."

The car descends into the private underground parking structure. "Any idea what this meeting's actually about?"

"Three guesses, and the first two don't count." Penn studies me carefully. "Your little obsession with Aurora Harrison has Jax concerned about your priorities."

"My priorities are perfectly aligned."

"Are they? Because from where I'm sitting, you're risking a multi-billion-dollar arrangement with Derek Harrison over a piece of—"

I cut him off with a look that has made grown men lose control of their bladders. "Choose your next words carefully."

Penn raises his hands in mock surrender. "Easy, tiger. Just pointing out the obvious. Jax isn't wrong to question your judgment here."

The Vipers' headquarters beneath the old Westside theater is dimly lit as always, the underground command center humming with activity. Jax sits at the head of the obsidian conference table, his fingers steepled beneath his chin as Penn and I take our seats.

"Gentlemen." Jax's voice carries without effort. "I'm pleased you could join us on such short notice."

"Security protocols for tonight's masquerade," Jax begins, his eyes never leaving mine. "I understand you've implemented... extraordinary measures, Hunter."

"Standard procedure for an event of this profile." My voice remains even.

Jax's lips curl into something approximating a smile. "Fifteen armed men seem excessive unless you're expecting trouble." He leans forward slightly. "Or perhaps protecting something particularly valuable."

The implication hangs between us. I maintain my composure while mentally reviewing contingency plans. If Jax makes a move against Aurora tonight, I'll need immediate countermeasures.

"In my experience," Jax continues, "distractions during critical operations lead to vulnerabilities. Vulnerabilities lead to failure." He glances meaningfully at the others. "The organization cannot afford either."

"My focus remains absolute," I reply, meeting his gaze without hesitation.

After the meeting concludes, I pull Penn aside in the secure communication room.

"I need you to deliver something to Aurora before tonight." I withdraw a velvet jewelry box from my pocket and open it, revealing an elegant diamond necklace.

Penn whistles. "Expensive insurance policy."

"The central pendant contains a tracking device," I explain, closing the box. "If anything happens tonight—"

"You'll know exactly where she is," Penn finishes. "Smart."

"With Jax escalating his surveillance, she needs protection." I hand him the box. "Deliver it personally. Tell her it's a gift for the ball. Don't mention the tracker."

Penn pockets the box. "And if she asks questions?"

"Tell her I'll explain everything tonight."

I wait until Penn exits with the jewelry box before making my move. With two hours remaining before the masquerade, it's time to test the waters.

I find Blaze first, cleaning his custom Glock in the weapons room.

"Jax seems on edge lately," I say casually, examining a tactical knife from the wall display.

Blaze's hands never pause in their practiced movements. "You noticed that too."

"The surveillance on Aurora. The emergency meetings. It feels... desperate."

He reassembles the firing pin before looking up. "Leaders who feel threatened make mistakes." He doesn't elaborate further, but the implication hangs between us.

In the monitoring center, Grayson reviews security footage with cold efficiency.

"The Marcus Chen situation," I begin, referencing Jax's former right-hand man. "Was that truly necessary?"

Grayson's eyes remain fixed on his screens. "Efficient, perhaps. Necessary? No." He pauses a beat too long. "Jax's definition of loyalty has narrowed considerably in recent months."

"And if definitions continue to narrow?"

"Then eventually, no one meets the criteria." Grayson finally turns to face me. "Even you."

I find Ari in the social operations center, reviewing dossiers for tonight's event.

"These additional security measures for the Vipers," I say, sliding into the chair opposite him. "An overreaction, wouldn't you say?"

Ari's elegant fingers tap the table twice, his nervous tell. "Jax believes himself infallible these days. Questioning his judgment has... consequences."

"And your assessment?"

"My assessment?" Ari's smile is diplomatic, practiced. "Is that the organization functions best when power is balanced." He leans forward slightly. "Recent events suggest the scales may have tipped too far in one direction."

I don't push further. I don't need to. The message is clear in what remains unsaid.

None will openly stand against Jax yet. But the fractures are there, hairline cracks in their loyalty that could split wide open given the right pressure. And when forced to choose sides, I know exactly where they'll stand.

Not with Jax. With me.

My phone vibrates as I leave the monitoring center. It's Grayson.

"We have a situation," he says the moment I answer.

"Elaborate." I move to a more private corner of the corridor.

"Jax has personally added fifteen names to the guest list for tonight's masquerade. Unknown entities. Not in our database."

My grip tightens on the phone. "When?"

"Within the last hour. And there's more. His private security detail has been conducting movement drills in the east quadrant of the property. Unusual formations, advanced tactical positioning. My source says they're practicing extraction protocols."

"Send me everything you have on the new additions."

"Already done." Grayson pauses. "Hunter... these aren't standard security measures for a social event."

I end the call and immediately pull up the encrypted files on my phone. Fifteen names, no digital footprint, no connection to our existing networks. This isn't a coincidence.

For the first time since setting this plan in motion, doubt creeps in. The image of Aurora walking into this viper's nest—quite literally—makes something cold settle in my chest. She doesn't understand what she's stepping into. What I've pulled her into.

I think of her standing at the cliff edge in the rain, vulnerable yet defiant. The way she looked at me in her kitchen, knife in hand, terrified but refusing to back down. Every instinct I have screams to protect what's mine, to keep her close where I can shield her.

But bringing her here, into this world of violence and ruthless power plays—am I protecting her or endangering her?

For a moment, I consider canceling her invitation, creating distance between us until I've neutralized Jax. The safest option would be to push her away entirely.

The thought makes something primal and possessive rise within me. No. She's mine. I just need to ensure her safety without compromising my position.

I dial Penn. "Change of plans."

27

AURORA

"What about this one?" Daisy holds up a midnight blue gown with silver beading across the bodice.

I blink, realizing I've been staring at the same rack of dresses for five minutes without seeing any of them. "It's nice."

"You've said that about the last three dresses I've shown you." Daisy narrows her eyes. "What's going on with you today? You've been a million miles away."

"Just tired." I turn to another rack, running my fingers over the fabrics without really seeing them.

"Aurora." Daisy's voice softens as she moves to stand beside me. "Talk to me. This isn't just about finding a dress for some masquerade, is it?"

My phone buzzes in my purse. I know without looking it's Hunter. Again. My stomach flips with equal parts excitement and dread.

"I'm fine." I pull out a black dress with a plunging neckline. "Maybe this one?"

Daisy takes the dress from my hands and hangs it back up. "Is it Hunter?"

The question hits like a slap. I freeze, unable to meet her eyes.

"I've seen how you look when your phone buzzes. I'm not stupid, Aurora."

"It's complicated," I whisper, finally looking up at her.

"He's engaged to your sister. That's not complicated—that's wrong." Her voice remains gentle despite her words.

I move toward a fitting room, grabbing a deep red gown on my way. "There are things you don't understand."

Daisy follows, leaning against the fitting room door as I change. "Then help me understand. Because from where I'm standing, you're playing with fire."

The zipper sticks halfway up my back. "He doesn't love her," I say quietly. "It's a business arrangement. Olivia told me herself."

"And that makes it okay?" Daisy's reflection appears behind mine in the mirror as she helps with the zipper. Her eyes find mine. "Even if it's just business, what happens when Olivia finds out? What happens to your family?"

I turn to face the mirror, the red dress clinging to my curves like it was made for me. Hunter would love it. The thought brings both pleasure and shame.

"You're falling for him, aren't you?" Daisy's voice is barely audible.

I don't answer, but my silence is confirmation enough.

Daisy sighs and sits on the small bench in the fitting room. "Aurora, look at me."

I can't. Instead, I smooth imaginary wrinkles from the red dress, focusing on the way the fabric catches the light rather than my friend's concerned expression.

"Are you in love with Hunter Reed?"

The question hangs in the air between us. My throat tightens. I should deny it immediately, should laugh it off as ridiculous. But the words won't come.

"I don't..." My voice cracks. "I don't know what this is."

"That's not a no." Daisy's reflection watches me with quiet intensity.

I press my palms against the cool mirror and close my eyes. "It wasn't supposed to happen."

"But it did."

I nod, feeling tears threatening. "I've tried to stop it, Daisy. I've told him we can't. I've walked away. But then..."

"But then he pulls you back in," she finishes for me.

"It's not just him." I turn to face her, needing her to understand. "Something happens when we're together. Something I can't control. I've never felt anything like it."

Daisy reaches for my hand. "You can't deny it anymore, can you?"

"No." The admission feels like both surrender and relief. "I can't."

"Oh, Aurora." Her fingers tighten around mine. There's no judgment in her eyes, only worry.

"What am I going to do?" I whisper, the reality of my situation crashing down around me.

My phone rings with Olivia's custom tone, cutting through the heavy silence between Daisy and me. My stomach drops.

"It's her," I whisper, staring at my purse like it contains a venomous snake.

Daisy gives me a pointed look. "You should answer it."

With trembling fingers, I retrieve my phone. Olivia's smiling face fills the screen as I accept the video call.

"Aurora! Finally! I've been trying to reach you all morning." Olivia's face is radiant, her perfectly styled hair bouncing as she moves. "Are you shopping? Did you find something for the masquerade yet? Please tell me you're actually coming."

"I—yes, we're looking at dresses." I angle the camera up slightly to hide the red gown I'm wearing, the one that made me think of Hunter.

"Show me what you're trying! I'm dying to see." She's practically vibrating with excitement.

"Nothing worth showing yet." I force a smile. "What's up?"

"You won't believe what just arrived!" She disappears from frame momentarily before reappearing with an ornate gold mask decorated with crystals and peacock feathers. "Hunter had it custom-made! Isn't it divine?"

"It's beautiful," I manage, feeling Daisy's eyes burning into my back.

"And that's not all!" Olivia continues, oblivious to my discomfort. "Hunter's arranged for the entire top floor of Reed Technologies to be transformed. There's going to be acrobats suspended from the ceiling, a fifteen-piece orchestra, and apparently some surprise at midnight that even I don't know about!"

I watch my sister's animated face as she describes the event in elaborate detail, her eyes bright with excitement over a party being thrown by the man I've been sleeping with behind her back.

"You have to come, Aurora. It won't be the same without you there."

Guilt coils in my stomach like a living thing. "I wouldn't miss it," I lie.

I end the call and set my phone down on the bench beside me, exhaling a shaky breath. The guilt sits heavy in my chest, making it hard to breathe. Olivia's excitement about Hunter's masquerade ball and him as her fiancé cuts deeper than any knife could.

"You can't do this to yourself." Daisy's voice pulls me back to the present. She's standing there with a dress I hadn't noticed before—a stunning black gown with a sweetheart neckline and delicate crystal beading that trails down like stars against a night sky. The fabric looks like liquid shadow, designed to move like water with each step.

"When did you find that?" I ask, reaching out to touch the smooth material.

"While you were on the phone. And don't change the subject." Daisy holds the dress against me, her eyes serious despite the beautiful gown between us. "This is perfect for you. But more importantly, Aurora, you need to tell Olivia tonight."

My hand drops from the dress. "Tonight?"

"Yes, tonight. This has gone on long enough." Her voice is gentle but firm. "Every day you wait makes it worse. You saw how excited she is about this party, and about a future with a man who's sleeping with her sister."

The words sting with their truth. I turn away from the mirror, unable to look at my own reflection. "I know."

"Do you? Because this isn't just about you and Hunter anymore. It's about Olivia, who deserves better than this deception." Daisy places the dress carefully on the hook and takes both my hands in hers. "It can't go on any longer, Aurora. You know that."

I close my eyes, picturing Olivia's radiant face as she showed off the mask Hunter had custom-made for her. The same Hunter who whispered in my ear last night that I was the only one he wanted. The same Hunter, who is still technically her fiancé.

"You're right," I finally say, opening my eyes to meet Daisy's concerned gaze. "I'll tell her tonight."

"I'll tell her tonight," I say again, this time with more conviction. The weight of the decision settles over me, both burden and relief.

Daisy hands me the black gown. "Try this one."

I slip it on, the cool fabric sliding against my skin like water. Daisy zips me up and steps back.

"Oh," she whispers.

I turn to the mirror and catch my breath. The dress transforms me. The beading captures the light with each subtle movement, like stars appearing and disappearing in the night sky. The bodice hugs my curves, then flows into a skirt that seems to float around my legs.

"This is the one," Daisy says behind me.

I nod, unable to speak. In this dress, I feel both powerful and vulnerable.

My mind races ahead to the masquerade. I'll arrive early, before the crowds. I'll find Olivia alone, pull her into one of the quiet corners away from prying eyes. I'll start with how much I love her, how she deserves honesty above all else.

The words form in my head: *Olivia, there's something I need to tell you about Hunter and me...*

But then what? How do I explain that her sister betrayed her? That the man she's engaged to has been in my bed? That I've fallen for him despite knowing it was wrong from the very beginning?

I smooth my hands down the front of the dress, watching the crystals catch the light. Maybe I should start with Hunter's feelings first. *The engagement isn't what you think. Hunter doesn't want to marry you. He wants to be with me.*

No, that sounds horrible, like I'm placing blame on her.

I practice another approach in my head: *I need to tell you something that will hurt you, and I'm so sorry. Hunter and I have been seeing each other.*

Simple. Direct. Honest.

The dress moves with me as I shift my weight, perfectly balanced between elegant and striking. I'll wear this tonight when I finally tell the truth.

28

HUNTER

I scan the ballroom from behind my obsidian mask, cataloging every entrance, exit, and security position. My men are stationed where they should be with two at each door, three circulating through the crowd, and five more monitoring from concealed positions in the mezzanine. The earpiece tucked discreetly beneath my mask buzzes with regular status updates.

"East entrance clear."

"Northwest balcony secured."

"No sign of additional personnel beyond authorized list."

I acknowledge each report with subtle finger taps against my champagne flute while maintaining the facade of the charming host. New York City's elite mill about in their finery, faceless behind elaborate masks, unaware of the currents running beneath this carefully orchestrated spectacle.

"Mr. Reed, such a magnificent event," purrs the wife of Judge Carlton, her peacock feather mask bobbing as she speaks.

I offer her a smile I've perfected for these occasions. "You're too kind."

My attention never wavers from Jax, who stands across the room in a silver wolf mask that does nothing to disguise the predator beneath. He's surrounded by his personal security detail. All of them are men I don't recognize. Not Vipers. Outsiders.

A ripple moves through the crowd near the main entrance. The sea of guests' parts, and I freeze.

Aurora.

She steps into the ballroom in a midnight-black gown that clings to her body like a second skin, crystals cascading down the fabric like stars falling through darkness. Her mask is black with lace patterns, covering just enough to make her mysterious while leaving the lower half of her face exposed.

For one unguarded moment, I forget about Jax, about the Vipers, about the danger surrounding us. I forget everything except the sight of her.

I force myself back to reality, discreetly activating the tracking app on my phone. The diamond necklace is in pride of place around her neck. Good. If anything happens, I'll know exactly where she is.

I move through the crowd, acknowledging guests with enough attention to satisfy their egos, not enough to invite extended conversation. My target never wavers: Aurora.

When we finally converge near the ornate ice sculpture, I extend my hand formally. "Miss Harrison, I'm delighted you could attend."

She places her hand in mine, her fingers trembling beneath my grip. To anyone watching, we're simply host and guest exchanging pleasantries. The perfect picture of propriety.

I lean forward, my lips brushing her ear as I turn her slightly, positioning my back to Jax's line of sight. My voice drops to barely a whisper.

"Stay visible. Don't go anywhere alone. If we're separated, find Penn immediately."

Her eyes widen behind her mask, but she recovers, offering a polite smile. "The event is magnificent, Mr. Reed."

"The necklace suits you," I say, my fingers brushing the diamond tracking device at her throat. I release her hand and step back, my public persona firmly in place. "Please, enjoy the evening."

Throughout the next hour, I maintain constant awareness of two things: Aurora's position and Jax's movements. The pattern becomes unmistakable. Whenever Aurora shifts to a new location, Jax adjusts his position accordingly.

He's watching her.

When Aurora joins a circle of socialites near the string quartet, Jax abandons his conversation with Senator Mitchell—a man whose campaign he personally financed—to casually drift in her direction.

My jaw clenches as Jax approaches her, offering a champagne flute, which she accepts with obvious hesitation.

This is unprecedented. Jax typically ignores members' partners, viewing them as liabilities or, at best, convenient facades. Yet here he is, engaging Aurora in what appears to be an animated conversation, his silver wolf mask tilted attentively toward her.

I intercept Penn near the eastern bar. "What the fuck is happening?"

Penn's eyes track my concern to where Jax stands

entirely too close to Aurora. "Never seen him give two shits about a woman before. Not like this."

"Keep your people on him. I want to know if he so much as breathes in her direction when I'm not looking."

Something's off.

I track one of Jax's security personnel. He's a broad-shouldered man with military bearing, abandoning his post near the champagne fountain to reposition himself beside the northeast exit. Three minutes later, another one shifts to cover the service corridor leading to the kitchen. Within fifteen minutes, I count six personnel changes, all centralizing control over the room's escape routes.

"Hunt," Penn's voice crackles through my earpiece. "We've identified fifteen guests not on the approved list."

I spot one immediately. A woman in a crimson dress and raven mask. Her posture is too alert. When she brushes past Senator Harlow, her hand briefly touches his lower back, checking for a weapon.

"They're running counter-surveillance," I murmur into my concealed mic. "These aren't socialites. They're operatives."

My focus snaps back to Aurora, currently engaged in conversation with Ari near the east balcony. Relief floods through me when I see Ari's protective stance—he's keeping her visible while blocking direct approaches. Good man.

I begin making my way toward them, maintaining a casual pace despite the urgency building in my chest. Aurora laughs at something Ari says, the sound momentarily cutting through the tension coiling inside me.

Three steps from reaching them, a hand clamps onto my shoulder.

"Hunter." Jax's voice carries the illusion of warmth. "I've been looking for you."

I turn to find him flanked by two of his new security personnel. The silver wolf mask does nothing to hide the calculation in his eyes.

"Senator Blackwell has been asking for you," Jax continues smoothly. "Something about the military contract we discussed last quarter. He insists it's critical we speak immediately."

My gaze flicks to Aurora, now watching our interaction with visible concern.

"Surely it can wait," I reply, keeping my tone even. "I was just about to—"

"It cannot." Jax's fingers dig harder into my shoulder. "The senator has arranged a private meeting room. We should join him now."

I weigh my options rapidly. Refusing Jax directly would escalate whatever game he's playing. But leaving Aurora vulnerable isn't acceptable either.

"Of course," I tell Jax, maintaining perfect composure despite the rage building inside me. "I'll join you shortly. First, let me inform Mr. Carter about a security adjustment."

Jax's fingers tighten fractionally on my shoulder. "I'm sure your staff can handle any adjustments."

I stare directly into the eyes behind his silver wolf mask. "This requires my personal attention. Two minutes."

Without waiting for his response, I move toward Ari and Aurora, feeling Jax's gaze burning into my back. Ari reads the situation immediately as I approach, his posture shifting subtly into defensive mode.

"Ari," I say loudly enough for nearby guests to hear,

"there's an issue with the east wing lighting. Would you handle it?"

Understanding flickers in his eyes. "Of course."

I turn to Aurora, keeping my expression neutral for our audience. "Miss Harrison, I apologize, but urgent business requires my attention. Mr. Carter will ensure you have everything you need."

I let my hand brush hers, voice dropping to a whisper. "Don't leave his side. No matter what."

Aurora nods slightly, fear flickering behind her mask. "I understand."

Turning to Ari, I murmur, "Keep her safe. No one approaches her. Not even Jax."

"With my life," he promises quietly.

I reluctantly walk away, joining Jax and his security detail at the edge of the ballroom.

As we reach the corridor, I glance back over my shoulder. Jax gives me a predatory smile as he moves behind me, his silver mask gleaming under the chandeliers.

A chill runs through me as the truth crystallizes. This isn't random. The entire evening has been orchestrated to separate me from Aurora at precisely this moment. Whatever Jax is planning, it's going to happen while he has me detained in some bullshit meeting. I have to trust that Ari can handle it.

29

AURORA

The moment Ari and I are alone, my eyes scan the crowded ballroom, heart hammering against my ribs. Hunter's warning echoes in my mind, his urgency unsettling me. That's when I spot her—Olivia, radiant in her cream gown, the custom mask Hunter designed framing her eyes perfectly.

"There's Liv," I tell Ari, already moving toward her. "I need to speak with her."

He follows closely. "Hunter said to stay with you."

"Then tag along," I reply, weaving through elegantly dressed bodies. "But give us some space when I talk to her."

Olivia's face brightens when she sees me approaching. "Aurora! Finally! I've been looking everywhere for you." She twirls, her dress catching the light. "What do you think? Does the mask work with the dress? Hunter had it specially made."

The guilt twists deeper in my stomach at the mention of his name.

"You look stunning," I say honestly. "The belle of the ball."

She laughs, squeezing my hand. "Says the woman in that incredible black gown. You're turning more heads than I am."

"Please. This old thing?" I gesture dramatically at my dress, falling into our familiar pattern of banter.

"Oh, stop. I saw at least three executives nearly walk into walls watching you cross the room." She lowers her voice conspiratorially. "Including that gorgeous VP from Hunter's R&D department."

I force a smile, my resolve strengthening. "Speaking of Hunter... Liv, I need to talk to you about something."

Her expression shifts to concern. "What's wrong? You look serious."

"Not here," I say, scanning the crowded ballroom. "Somewhere private."

I spot a small alcove tucked behind a massive floral arrangement, partially hidden from the main room but still within sight of Ari. Perfect.

"Come with me," I say, taking her hand and guiding her toward the alcove.

"You're scaring me," Olivia says as we move away from the crowd. "Is everything okay?"

"Just... something important we need to discuss," I manage, my heart pounding as I lead her into the secluded space.

Once we're tucked into the alcove, all my carefully rehearsed words evaporate. Olivia stands before me, eyes bright and trusting behind her beautiful mask.

"What's this about, Aurora?" She tilts her head, sensing my discomfort.

I take a deep breath, my fingers instinctively finding the diamond necklace Hunter gave me. "It's about Hunter."

"Is something wrong with the engagement?" Concern crosses her features.

"Liv, I've been sleeping with Hunter." The words tumble out unfiltered. "We almost kissed before the engagement was announced, but... It's continued since then."

Olivia goes completely still. For a moment, I wonder if she heard me. Then I see her eyes widen behind her mask, pupils dilating.

"You're joking." Her voice comes out flat. "This is some sick joke."

"I wish it were." The guilt claws at my throat. "I never meant for it to happen. We met that day at my dad's cliff house when I was standing near the edge—"

"Stop." One gloved hand raises between us. "You expect me to believe my sister and my fiancé have been having an affair this entire time?"

"When he approached Dad about the engagement, he had believed after we met at my dad's old house that I was Olivia Harrison. It was a misunderstanding."

Her laugh cuts me off, sharp and brittle. "A misunderstanding? And what about these weeks, where you've continued while I plan our wedding? You should have told me!"

"Liv, please—"

"My own sister." Her disbelief crystallizes into something harder, colder. "All those times you helped me plan the wedding. All those conversations about Hunter." Her voice drops to a whisper. "You sat there and watched me talk about him while knowing..."

The color drains from her face, replaced by a spreading flush. Her perfectly assembled composure slips, revealing rage I've rarely seen in my sister.

"You've always been like this," she says. "Taking what isn't yours."

Her eyes narrow behind the intricate mask, no longer the soft, forgiving sister I've known all my life. This Olivia is someone with ice in her veins.

"I was going to tell you," I say, my voice cracking at the edges. "That night when we were discussing your feelings toward him, I was planning to confess everything then."

Olivia's eyes narrow further, the beautiful mask now looking ominous against her hardened expression.

"Remember when we talked in your bedroom? You specifically told me you wouldn't be upset if the engagement was called off. If Hunter... if he wanted someone else." I reach for her arm, but she steps back. "You said it was just a business arrangement. That you didn't even love him."

"And that gave you permission?" She jerks her head, a sharp, disbelieving motion.

"No, of course not. But I thought... I thought maybe you'd understand—"

"Understand?" Her voice remains low but cuts like glass. "Let me be perfectly clear. I'm not upset that Hunter wants you. I never loved him. This arrangement was Dad's idea, not mine."

My breath catches with a flicker of hope.

"What I'm upset about," she continues, "is that my sister, the person I trust most in this world, has been sneaking around behind my back. Lying to my face. For weeks." She removes her mask, revealing eyes bright with unshed tears. "You sat with me planning a wedding while sleeping with my fiancé. You let me ramble about him while knowing..."

I reach for her again. "Liv—"

"No." She steps back. "It's the deceit, Aurora. The lies.

The way you both made a fool of me." Her composure slips for just a second, revealing the pain beneath her anger. "You could have told me. At any point, you could have been honest with me."

"I was afraid—"

"Of what? That I'd be upset you were sleeping with a man I don't even love? No." She shakes her head. "You were afraid I'd see you for who you really are. Someone who takes the easy path instead of the right one."

"When did it start?" Olivia demands, her voice rising. "How long have you been sneaking around behind my back?"

I stare at my feet, shame burning through me. "A week or so after the engagement announcement."

"A week?" She laughs bitterly. "So, while I was showing you wedding venues—"

"It wasn't planned, Liv. It just... happened."

"Things don't just happen, Aurora. You make choices." She steps closer, eyes flashing. "Did he seduce you? Is that what you're claiming?"

"No. Yes, it's complicated." I wrap my arms around myself. "At first, I tried to resist. I told him it was wrong, that you were my sister—"

"How noble of you," she cuts in, voice dripping with sarcasm. "And yet somehow you ended up in his bed anyway."

"We were drawn to each other from the first moment," I admit, the words painful in my throat. "I fought it, Liv, I swear I did. But every time I was around him..."

"Spare me the romance novel details." She spins away, then whirls back. "So what is this to you? A fling? An exciting forbidden affair? The thrill of taking what belongs to someone else?"

"It's not like that," I whisper, feeling tears threaten. "I never meant to hurt you. I never wanted any of this to happen."

"But it did happen. And you let it continue." Her eyes narrow. "Why?"

The question hangs between us. I could lie, minimize, or make excuses. But I owe her the truth.

"Because I fell in love with him," I confess, my voice breaking. "I didn't mean to, but I did. I love him, Liv."

Something changes in Olivia's face. The anger doesn't disappear; instead, it transforms, crystallizing into something colder. Her breathing steadies. Her shoulders relax. The flush fades from her cheeks.

"You love him," she repeats, her voice eerily calm. She studies me with a detached curiosity, as if seeing me clearly for the first time. "My sweet, impulsive sister… in love with Hunter Reed."

This new composure frightens me more than her outrage did. Her eyes remain fixed on mine.

"How interesting," she says. She adjusts her mask back into place. "Tell me, Aurora. Does he love you back?"

Olivia's question hangs between us. Does Hunter love me? The truth would only twist the knife deeper, so I hesitate, searching for words that won't hurt her more.

Before I can answer, movement at the edge of our alcove catches my eye. Ari stumbles toward us, his normally graceful movements uncoordinated and sluggish. His eyes are unfocused, his mask askew, and he's gripping the wall for support.

"Aurora," he slurs, reaching out. "Run…"

He collapses face-first onto the marble floor with a sickening thud.

"What the hell?" Olivia whispers, stepping backward.

Two men in server uniforms appear behind Ari. They are wearing earpieces, not masks, and the bulges beneath their jackets reveal concealed weapons.

"Ms. Harrison," one says, looking between us. "Both of you. Come with us quietly."

"Like hell," I snap, grabbing Olivia's arm and pulling her behind me.

Two more men emerge from behind, cutting off our exit. My hand flies to my clutch, fumbling for my phone.

"That won't be necessary," says the closest man, lunging forward.

I kick off my heels and slam one into his face. He grunts, stumbling back as blood spurts from his nose. Beside me, Olivia swings her heavy clutch, connecting with another man's temple.

"Help!" Olivia screams, but the music drowns her voice.

I feel a sharp prick in my shoulder. Turning, I see one of them pulling a syringe away. The room instantly begins to tilt.

"No," I gasp, legs buckling. I reach for Olivia, but my arm feels impossibly heavy.

Olivia's eyes widen in horror as another man grabs her from behind, pressing something to her neck. Her body goes rigid, then limp.

My vision blurs as they catch her falling form. There's a beeping sound as they sweep a device across my neck. "Fitted a tracker in the necklace," one man says, "Take it off her."

They open the clasp, and it gives way, clattering to the floor.

The diamond necklace containing Hunter's tracker is lost as rough hands drag me backward. I try to fight, to scream, but my mouth won't work.

"Both targets secured," someone says above me, voice distorted like I'm underwater.

Darkness creeps in from the edges of my vision. My last conscious thought is that Hunter won't know where to find us.

Hunter & Aurora's story continues in book 2 of the Hunter and Prey Duet, Vow of Venom.

You can order the book here or read it for FREE with a Kindle Unlimited subscription from January 18th.

One moment of brutal truth to my sister, and both our worlds collapsed into darkness.

The confession had barely left my lips—the truth about Hunter and me laid bare before Olivia—when men drugged us and dragged us from the masquerade's shadows. Her eyes, still wide with betrayal and shock from my revelation, were the last thing I saw before darkness claimed us both.

Now, captives in a nightmare neither of us created, Olivia and I face a twisted reality where our personal drama pales in comparison to the dangerous game surrounding us. The sister I betrayed has become my only ally in a prison designed to break us.

Hunter Reed—billionaire, secret Viper, the man who set my body and heart aflame—has transformed into something terrifying in his quest to reclaim us. We hear the men talk of how he is tearing through the city's underworld, sacrificing everything he built to find what he considers his.

As Olivia and I struggle to stay alive, bitter truths emerge from the shadows: my father's suicide was orchestrated, Olivia's engagement was strategic manipulation, and I, caught between family loyalty and passion, was always meant to be the catalyst for destruction.

With each passing hour in captivity, as Olivia processes my betrayal while fighting for our survival, I'm forced to question everything: Is Hunter fighting to save us both, or merely to possess what he claims as his own? And when forced to choose between my sister's forgiveness and Hunter's dangerous love, which path leads to salvation, and which to ruin?

This book concludes the Hunter and Prey duet, picking up directly after the cliffhanger of Vow of Malice. Contains dark themes, explicit scenes, and content that may disturb some readers.

ALSO BY BIANCA COLE

Beautiful Monsters Series
Stalk Me: A Dark Mafia Romance

Shatter Me: A Dark Mafia Romance

Chain Me: A Dark Captive Mafia Romance

Hunt Me: A Dark Mafia Romance

Once Upon a Villain
Pride: A Dark Arranged Marriage Romance

Hook: A Dark Forced Marriage Romance

Wicked: A Dark Forbidden Mafia Romance

Unhinged: A Dark Captive Cartel Romance

Beast: A Dark Billionaire Romance

Wolf: A Dark Primal Mafia Romance

The Syndicate Academy
Sinister Games: A Dark Forbidden Mafia Academy Romance

Cruel Bully: A Dark Mafia Academy Romance

Sinful Lessons: A Dark Forbidden Mafia Academy Romance

Twisted Games: A Dark Enemies to Lovers Forbidden Mafia Academy Romance

Chicago Mafia Dons
Cruel Savior: A Dark Forbidden Mafia Romance

Violent Leader: A Dark Enemies to Lovers Captive Mafia Romance

Evil Prince: A Dark Arranged Marriage Romance

Brutal Daddy: A Dark Captive Mafia Romance

Cruel Vows: A Dark Forced Marriage Mafia Romance

Dirty Secret: A Dark Enemies to Lovers Mafia Romance

Dark Crown: A Dark Arranged Marriage Romance

Boston Mafia Dons Series

Empire of Carnage: A Dark Captive Mafia Romance

Cruel Obsession: A Dark Mafia Arranged Marriage Romance

Savage Bidder: A Dark Captive Mafia Romance

Ruthless King: A Dark Forbidden Mafia Romance

Vicious Bond: A Dark Brother's Best Friend Mafia Romance

Wicked Captor: A Dark Captive Mafia Romance

New York Mafia DonsSeries

Her Irish Daddy: A Dark Mafia Romance

Her Russian Daddy: A Dark Mafia Romance

Her Italian Daddy: A Dark Mafia Romance

Her Cartel Daddy: A Dark Mafia Romance

Romano Mafia Brother's Series

Her Mafia Daddy: A Dark Daddy Romance

Her Mafia Boss: A Dark Romance

Her Mafia King: A Dark Romance

New York Brotherhood Series

Bought: A Dark Mafia Romance

Captured: A Dark Mafia Romance

Claimed: A Dark Mafia Romance

Bound: A Dark Mafia Romance

Taken: A Dark Mafia Romance

Forbidden Desires Series

Bryson: An Enemies to Lovers Office Romance

Logan: A First Time Professor And Student Romance

Ryder: An Enemies to Lovers Office Romance

Dr. Fox: A Forbidden Romance

Royally Mated Series

Her Faerie King: A Faerie Royalty Paranormal Romance

Her Alpha King: A Royal Wolf Shifter Paranormal Romance

Her Dragon King: A Dragon Shifter Paranormal Romance

Her Vampire King: A Dark Vampire Romance

ABOUT THE AUTHOR

I love to write stories about over the top alpha bad boys who have heart beneath it all, fiery heroines, and happily-ever-after endings with heart and heat. My stories have twists and turns that will keep you flipping the pages and heat to set your Kindle on fire.

For as long as I can remember, I've been a sucker for a good romance story. I've always loved to read. Suddenly, I realized why not combine my love of two things, books and romance?

My love of writing has grown over the past four years, and I now publish exclusively on Amazon, weaving stories about dirty mafia bad boys and the women they fall head over heels for.

If you enjoyed this book, please follow me on Amazon, Bookbub, or any of the below social media platforms for alerts when more books are released.

Printed in Dunstable, United Kingdom